Bus 59 and a Half

MEL INGRID

ISBN: 1719269289
ISBN-13: 978-1719269285

DEDICATION

This is for all the people who don't know why the hell their world is crashing down. This is for all the people who have a hard time getting out the bed in the morning. This is for all the people who are always there for the ones who need them.

This is for anyone who is struggling to find their calm in the midst of a hurricane.

CONTENTS

PROLOGUE

The plush upholstery, soft under his thighs.

Chipped red doors.

65.

Slick. Crunch. Rustle. Pow!

No time to search the whole world around.

Down, down, down.

His ears. His mouth. His lungs.

Those blue, blue veins on pale skin that used to be dark olive.

CHAPTER ONE

ALEXI

Summer Vacation: Day One

untitled

Whoever set it up didn't have a lot of patience–the first letter of the title was uncapitalized and the byline wasn't even close to legible. Heck, the entire thing was draped in a cloth, invisible to everyone (or lack thereof) who actually bothered to come to the exhibit.

The corners of her mouth curved into a lopsided smirk. She tossed the last of her tennis balls into her orange backpack and hoisted it up on her shoulders. In one quick movement, she closed the scorching wire gate behind her.

Alexi was going to commit a crime.

The trees looked like disoriented green blurs as she thundered across the abandoned parking lot. It was June 27, the last day of school, and the start of another summer. But the end of the school year didn't just mean soiling her no-felony reputation. It meant she was free from algebra classes that made learning about the Gulf War seem interesting were over. It was "good riddance" to five a.m. alarms. The absence of drama queen posses and two-week couples sucking face smushed against the lockers were bonus points.

Her hot, sticky limbs slapped against each other as she ran like a madman, her feet barely gripping the asphalt before she took another step. Through toffee bangs tangled together with sweat, Alexi squinted at the horizon. There was a dot in the distance. It appeared to be accelerating–towards her.

Is that a bike? Alexi's bag bounced up and down on her back as she ran. The dot grew larger. It *was* a bike. "Hey!" She yelped as it hurtled forward, stopping a few inches to close to her leg. The rubber spikes on the wheel scraped her skin, drawing a scratch.

"Oh shit, sorry," someone mumbled.

Alexi knew that voice more than she wanted to. She felt the humid air strangle her, burn her head. She panted. Her fingers curled into claws.

The boy with almond-shaped eyes that sparkled began to walk his bicycle away. His sneakers on the pavement made his getaway a loud one. He didn't get far when Alexi caught one of the handles. Reid flinched when she did, tensing up in his goody-two-shoes way, all innocent. Like he was.

"Well, well, well," Alexi dragged each *well*, except it sounded more like *wHAle, wHAle, wHAle* through her heavy breaths. She cocked her head to the side slightly, raising both of her eyebrows. "Look who decided to liven up my day with their *oh-so-wonderful* presence."

"Oh, hi bean," Reid chuckled, pretending to be nonchalant. "You're bleeding." He ran his hand over her ankle and showed Alexi bright red drips congealed on his fingertips. She was, in fact, producing a rather alarming amount of blood–enough to stain the hem of her socks.

"You lied," Alexi spat. "You said you didn't have time after school, yet here you are acting all casual and stuff like you don't know what I'm talking about. Why did you tell me you were going to be busy if you weren't?" She demanded, frustration creasing her forehead. "I mean, I know I'm not your mom or anything and I don't have to know what you're doing or where you are all the time, but…" Annoyance tugged at her. She started to wring her hands to avoid having them wring something else. "You have time. You said you didn't have time!"

"I'm sorry! I forgot I had that police interview thing scheduled."

"No. You're not. You made me look like a fool waiting there after school. You didn't even text me. I felt like a lost puppy," she narrowed her eyes. "I don't want people to think I'm a lost puppy!"

Reid reached his hand out to calm her down but Alexi swiped him away.

"What does it matter what people think of you?" He asked. "It's the last day of school anyway."

"Well, it matters because I'm not Alexi at school. I'm the girl who got the whole class suspended because Grade-A asshole Jason Bhatia blamed that stupid April Fool's prank on me."

"Dude. It was a harmless prank. And it's June now."

"He recruited the half of the whole class to help him prank *our chemistry teacher* and *I wasn't even a part of it!*" Alexi pushed her sliding rectangle glasses up the bridge of her nose. "Plus, people still remember it." The afternoon was getting more intense now, the sun shifting to a position that was almost blinding. "You know what?" Alexi ran a hand through her coarse pixie cut. "I don't really care because you obviously think it's fine to lie to someone."

Reid rubbed the back of his neck, nibbling his lip with a grim expression.

"You *know* why I'm angry," she added.

Reid elected not to speak.

"Fine," Alexi huffed. Without a second glance, she sprinted off towards to the exhibit.

After what felt like decades of the sun burning her flesh, Alexi stumbled into the exhibit. The cool air conditioning welcomed her, soothing her chaffed thighs. She loved how the smell of the place became familiar over time–it was like she had known lemon air freshener and old potpourri since forever.

The exhibit wasn't exactly the most appealing or ideal venue. The paint on the walls peeled, and it disintegrated to dust at a light touch of the fingertips. A tiny army of house spiders inhabited the cracks at the foot of the wall. But the metaphor of not judging a book by its cover applied to it perfectly. The artwork enraptured her even after seeing it a million times.

She took a swig of her water bottle. "Ugh, why is it still so hot in here?" She whispered to no one in particular.

"It could just be me, you know," someone whispered back with a tease to his words.

"Please," Alexi guffawed. "That line is *so* old."

It was College Hottie, one of the regulars. He wore the same university hoodie every time she saw him, despite the weather. On most days, he arrived at the sculpture exhibit before Alexi did. A woman in dress clothes would accompany him on Wednesday and Friday evenings, and they would sit in the chairs talking.

The person across the room was who Alexi dubbed Flower Woman. Tall, elegant, smelled like expensive coffee. Alexi imagined her as the girly-girl type–princesses, dragons, magical kingdoms. It was also probably safe to assume she was also a compulsive clean freak. On one occasion, Alexi caught her picking up a random bottle of water lying on the ground using a tissue and clean her hands using hand sanitizer *three times* after she threw it into the trash can.

Alexi considered herself one of the regulars as well. She came here every day after school, 3:15 in the afternoon on non-tennis days, close to 5:00 when she was accompanied with a sack of neon yellow balls and a racket.

She began to wander around in the exhibit, pausing every now and then to admire a piece, when in reality, all she was thinking of was *untitled.* At last, she got to the corner where she would break the rules. If they wanted her to be in trouble, she would get herself into it.

Do not touch, said the cardboard sign. *Security cameras in operation.* Alexi wondered why someone would put something they didn't want people to see in a room designated for viewing. Every single time temptation cursed her, urging her to lift the cloth that shrouded the sculpture, see past that faint outline. Checking left and right to ensure that no one was looking at her, Alexi's fingers grasped the hem of the cloth. She held her breath, prepared to yank it off. "One," she chanted to herself, excitement bubbling inside her. "Two…"

The door swung open. Alexi let go. A pair of clumpy footsteps followed, each one making her more nervous.

"You're late today," someone commented. "It's 4:53. After school activity?"

Alexi turned around. Standing a few feet away from her was a middle-aged man with dark olive skin and gleaming brown irises. His hands had calluses visible from where she was standing. Vivid splashes of paint decorated his clothes. Mauve shadows cloaked his eyes. "Who are you and why are you stalking me?" She leaped to her defense right away.

The man and his two chins chuckled. "I could ask you the same."

"What?"

"Your foot," the man said instead. He pointed at her left ankle. The blood had long dried, but the wound was still moist and open, begging for an infection.

"Whatever," Alexi replied. "And why, exactly, have you been stalking me?" Her stance remained alert. Her eyes flitted towards the exit.

"You come here every day. You're probably fifteen. Sixteen, perhaps." The man ignored her question, moving closer to her.

Alexi took a step back, unzipping her backpack. She took out her tennis racket.

"Oh, we don't want to do that. You're going to bump into it." The man gestured at *untitled,* which she had been close to crashing into.

Alexi slid to the side.

"You play tennis, evidently. You must be sore then, what, with all that batting and swatting." He grabbed her wrist with his stare still trained on her gray eyes. His fingers were rough on her soft flesh.

Alexi jerked away. "Don't. Touch. Me."

"Apologies," the man drew back. "You have a lot of persistence," he remarked. "It's been two weeks since this place has opened and yet every time I pass you, you're always in front of that sculpture. Want to sneak a peek, huh?"

Alexi swallowed before settling on, "what did my wrist have to do with my persistence?"

The tune of an ice cream truck signaled little kids' delighted shrieks outside. Her heart rate slowed, her wariness boiled back into rage. She would not be here right now facing a strange stalker man if Reid had kept his promise. She would've been at the campsite by now, toasting marshmallows over a crackling fire or pitching a tent.

"You come here every day," the man proceeded to dismiss her questions. "I know why you do." He got her at that, she had to admit.

"I'm not going to answer any of your questions until you tell me who you are," she cautioned and raised the racket a little. What the hell did this guy want from her?

"Yusuf Bates," he extended his right hand. It was covered in bandages. "It's a pleasure to meet you."

Alexi shook his hand tentatively. "So what's your deal?"

The twinkle in Yusuf's eyes remained as if he were amused by how wary she was. "I have something for you to do during the summer. Would you like to apply for a job?"

"A job?" Alexi echoed.

"It's just for one day. It's a modeling position," Yusuf replied. He nodded towards the bulletin board on the wall. "This." There was a piece of light blue paper tacked to the cork, with "MODELS WANTED" printed on the top in a block font.

"Models wanted?"

The man nodded and reached into his shirt pocket, taking out a black business card with a white border. "Go to this website and fill out the form. No other requirements."

Alexi eyed the card, intrigued.

Don't trust strangers, her parents coached her. That rule felt so satisfying to disobey. This opportunity sounded better than committing a "crime" if she could even call it that. But Alexi wasn't going to let Yusuf string her along so easily if that was his intention.

"Do you run a company or something?" Alexi furrowed her brows. "Why are you offering me this?"

Yusuf smiled, baring all of his teeth in a Cheshire Cat-like grin.

"Who are you?"

"I'm the owner of this establishment and the sculptor of *untitled.*"

Alexi's eyes widened and checked the title card taped to the base of the sculpture. Sure enough, she could distinguish that *Y. Bates* had indeed been printed on it. "Oh my god."

Yusuf was already heading out of the exhibit.

"Hold on," Alexi went after him. "What's under *untitled?* Why is it covered? What's going to happen if someone were to touch it?"

Yusuf paused at the half-open door, shadows casting on the ground behind him. "You know, if you wanted to unveil it or steal it and sell it on the internet or do whatever you were planning to do, you should've just done it. There's just about nothing worse than indecisiveness," he said and left.

• • •

After Alexi got home and answered her parents' "how was your last day of school?" questions and listened to the consolations regarding her camping trip with Reid gone wrong during a baked ziti dinner, she took a shower.

With her hair still damp and the chafe marks on her inner thighs raw, Alexi settled into the teal beanbag in the corner of her room, her laptop balanced on her lap. "Cav... Bat... Sculptures dot com," she murmured to herself as she typed the link on the business card into the search engine, checking the business card Yusuf had given her. For a moment after she tapped enter, the entire screen was blank. Then the circle in the corner of the tab stopped spinning. Lines of text appeared.

MODELS WANTED

Interested in assisting us with an art competition? If you are, please apply here (www.cavbatsculptures.com/model-online-form/) for a chance to model for our three-piece collection to be presented at this year's SculptFest. Guidelines listed below.

"Hey mom," Alexi ran downstairs with her computer tucked underneath her arm. "I found a summer job!"

"That's nice," her mother replied from the kitchen. "What is it?"

Knowing that she would never be allowed to apply for anything outside of volunteer work or a job listed under the high school's summer community service hours program, Alexi lied. "Um, the art department is doing this thing."

"What's the thing?" Her mom turned off the faucet and turned around to face Alexi. It was terrifying how intense her stare was already. Alexi wondered what it would look like if she found out she wasn't telling the truth.

"Modeling for a sculpture contest. There's a partnership, apparently," she said, laying it on thick without thinking about what she was getting herself into. "It's extra credit. For those who want it."

Her mom dried her hands on her tomato sauce-stained apron. "Well, if you really want to, I guess. Anything I need to fill out?"

"Nope," Alexi grinned. She uncrossed her fingers behind her back. "I just need to let my art teacher know."

Her eyelids were heavy when her phone buzzed. Once, twice, three times… And it kept on going. Alexi groaned, squirming in her fetus sleeping position. The noise it made was a custom *bleep*– the one that told her it was Reid. "Fuck off," she mumbled in her pillow, squeezing her eyes shut.

But now she couldn't fall asleep. Not when her best friend ditched her for a stupid interview when it was possible that today was their last day together. For the past month, most of the conversations she and her family had during dinner were about transferring schools and moving. How it would be more convenient for her dad's job if they moved. How "nice" it would be to stay at her aunt's place when they went house hunting. How change was going to give her "a new perspective on life".

Alexi had only known Reid for one school year, but it made the friendships she had before feel like nothing. He was the only person who truly got her, locked the secrets she told him in a bulletproof safe. The guy respected her major league baseball opinions.

Friends like that don't last after someone leaves. It's a one in a million chance if they do. After you find a new crowd, you get sucked into a different wormhole in a different environment, and whatever history you had before would cease to exist.

That's why no apology from Reid would bring her back to normal any time soon. Better to leave with no attachments than a lingering connection.

CHAPTER TWO

DANA
Announcement Day of the Cardboard Boxes

Her hand moved across the canvas in quick, deft strokes. The fabric sagged, burdened with several layers of acrylic paint suffocating it. Dana wiped her forehead with the back of her palm. She dropped her brush in an old jam jar containing cloudy water. Picking up her fingerprint-smudged phone, she dialed her brother. "Don't get dinner," Dana told Ace the moment he picked up.

Dana's boyfriend, Robbie came out of the bathroom with a damp stubble and a neat line of tiny whiteheads dotting his jawline. His large mouth curved into a smile as he sat down in the pre-loved armchair in the corner. Mango, the family dog, plopped on Robbie's lap and nestled his head into the crook of his armpit.

"But Dee," Ace protested on the other end. "You said I could go buy—"

"Forget what I said earlier. I'm cooking tonight," Dana responded, standing up. She moved her art supplies and the mini potted succulents off of the patterned tablecloth, patting it smooth. "*Robbie's staying for dinner tonight,*" she whispered in a hushed voice, grinning so big that the top row of her teeth ground her bottom lip. Dana glanced over. Robbie was rubbing Mango's potbelly, close to dozing off. The ink-colored French bulldog whined.

"*Ooh, Mr. White Privilege is staying for dinner tonight,*" Ace said in a high-pitched voice, mocking her.

"Shut up," Dana rolled her eyes while watering the lilac solanum vines creeping down the balcony window. "Just because he's part German doesn't mean you get to ridicule him for it. Half of your *friends,*" Dana made air quotes when she said friends, although Ace couldn't see her, "are white anyway. And what's the problem being white? Or black or brown or–"

"Okay, yeah, *mom,* I get it," Ace groaned. "Jeez, can you like, not pick on everything I say?" Dana could hear him kick pebbles on the ground. His free hand was probably stuck in the hoodie he never washed. His ever-present slouch that never failed to accompany him made him look like a sleep-deprived turtle.

"He's my boyfriend," she clarified. "I love him."

"As if I don't know that," Ace replied, letting out a dry chuckle. "But just because he is doesn't mean he has to stay. Can't you two go to like a fancy restaurant or something? You make money, he's like rich or something, and I'd have the whole apartment to myself."

Dana ignored her brother and headed into the kitchen. A shock that sent her from her state of two a.m. Netflix to eight in the morning (post-coffee) hit her when her feet made contact with the cool tiles. "Fine," she admitted, wiggling her toes in delight. She had been painting in the humid living-slash-dining room for so long that she had grown accustomed to the steaming temperature. "Maybe you don't get along that well. But the only thing that makes it awkward–"

"Is if I think it is. Yeah, yeah."

Dana poked around in the fridge, scrounging for something other than nuke-able TV dinners. Her nose scrunched up at something looked like an avocado going bad in a plastic bag. She pulled open a compartment. "Fried rice and uh… garden salad? I got that Italian dressing you like when I swung by the supermarket yesterday."

"I had fried rice yesterday," Ace complained, but Dana could tell how grateful he was.

Ever since she and Robbie started to go out, she began to neglect to do a lot of things, like housework. Ace, who hated anything involving a sponge and window cleaner, had pitched in a lot more lately. It made Dana feel bad, but at least he wasn't leaving all the responsibilities to her anymore. Working nine to five at the police station was exhausting. And it provided an excuse for nights ending with grease-covered pizza and MSG-induced bathroom trips.

"Anyway, I gotta go," Dana struggled to turn the rusty faucet with her phone sandwiched between her shoulder and ear. "Are you taking the bus or the train?"

"Neither, actually," Ace said. "Homeboy's got a ride home this time. It's carpoolin' with the guys. Hey, that rhymed."

Dana rocked her knife forwards and backward, mincing the cilantro. "No, it did not. And you are *not* going with those weed dealers or I'm going to tell mom you smoked in high school and that you still are."

"Hah, you made a pun."

Fwwp.

"You ball up that paper and throw that lighter and those drugs into the trash can right now." Dana oiled the pan on the stove.

"Oops–" the sound of her brother's voice became muffled, but she could still hear him giggling like the little devil he was. "Oh *tsss* no *tsss tsss* breaking–" The line went dead.

Dana sighed, exasperated.

Robbie moseyed into the kitchen and peered at the contents of her mug. He drank it. "Was that Ace?" He asked, playing with the ends of her apron strings.

"Oh, you mean that person I'm *totally* not related to?" Dana scraped the last bits of diced bell pepper stuck onto the cutting board with her knife into the frying pan. She reached her hand behind her and pawed the air until Robbie handed her the bottle of soy sauce. "Thanks."

A moment passed. It was quiet. Lots of quiet moments filled their relationship, ones that Dana didn't know how to feel about. Most of them were comfortable, but over time she began to wonder if it was because they were losing interest in each other.

"So are you sure you want to stay for dinner?" Dana questioned. A sparrow perched on the small bay window next to the small ceramic piggy bank. It had belonged to mom.

Live a good life, she had told both of them before they moved out, after a long speech on how they had to eat healthy and pay the rent on time. But was "good" this? Was "good" an apartment less than five hundred square feet, salty takeout suppers, bills ripped open and discarded on the table? Dana wasn't even sure that "good" equaled to happiness anymore.

"Dana," fingers snapped in front of her face, waking her from her sudden reverie.

"What? Oh," Dana looked down. "Ah, crap!" She grabbed the wooden spatula and raked through the rice. "Oh god, it's burnt." She turned off the heat. "You probably don't want to have dinner here now, do you?" She laughed, her stomach queasy with embarrassment.

Hi, I'd like to order a headstone. The epitaph, you say? "Couldn't even marry pizza because her forever alone-ness didn't limit her unfortunate fate to only humans."

"Hey, hey," Robbie chuckled. He hugged her from behind, his lanky frame curving into her much more voluptuous one. He massaged her shoulders. "I'm not going anywhere."

"You're just saying that because you haven't found the right moment to break up with me yet."

"What?" Robbie leaned down to meet her height. This was one of the times that it made Dana feel like a little kid. Pro tip: don't date someone nine inches taller than you. "Stop it with that self-deprecating crap." His green hooded eyes trailed from her face to the view outside. "Look how beautiful it is." It *was* beautiful. The sunset melted into their skin like butter, illuminating the dim room with hues of fuchsia and yellow. It made the coat of shine on the piggybank seem even brighter.

It made "good" feel less relevant.

All was fine. All was calm. All was not filled with tension. Broken double bass notes from Robbie's band's jazz CD played from Dana's computer.

It sounds great, she had reassured him. *If you compared it to a wolf going through puberty howling at a full moon.*

"Well, I don't know if Dana told you," Ace piped up, smoothie froth coating his upper lip. He licked it off like a ravenous dog while giving Robbie his Look.

Dana wanted to disappear.

"But I got a job," Ace pursed his lips and crossed his arms. "You know," he gestured with his hand. "Just some casual modeling. It's for this annual sculpture competition thing."

"You got a job?!" Dana stared at him wide-eyed.

"You would've known if you bothered to check your phone if you weren't so busy playing lip guitar with your *boyfriend,*" Ace spat. "Thanks for being such an awesome supporter."

"Look, I'm sorry! I had a really long work day and–"

The ceiling light flickered a few times before it went dark. The only source of light came from Ace's phone. "I think I should go," Robbie's feet shuffled getting up. He pushed in his chair. "Dinner was great. Congrats, Ace."

"Wait," Dana called.

"*Wait,*" Ace mimicked.

Dana elbowed him in the ribs.

"Ow!"

"How are you going to get home?" Dana scrambled to get up, managing to run into the electric fan atop the chair stacked high with secondhand college textbooks. It buzzed. "Yowch! Okay. Okay. It's past eleven. Your last bus left already. You could stay here for the night."

"I really shouldn't," Robbie said. He sounded apologetic. Giving Dana a quick kiss on her cheek, he ejected his band CD out of Dana's laptop and vacated the apartment.

Mango barked. It didn't chase the silence away. The siblings sat at the dining table, the fan whirring. Crumpling sounds punctured through the air when the blades hit the indented wire. The lights coming from the other homes across them darkened one by one. Crickets chirped.

Dana wanted to scream at Ace for ruining everything, always wanting to hog all the attention. But it was on her. She burned the food, she was the one who hardly cleaned anymore, and now she was the one who was going to screw his life up.

"I'm moving out."

• • •

80's keyboard synths traveled from Ace's room, *NSYNC's *Bye Bye Bye* playing. He always had the appropriate song for any occasion.

Black Nintendo in hand with *Legend of Zelda* paused on its screen, Ace shoved the door open.

Dana took it as an invitation.

He then proceeded to plunk back onto the bench below one of his movie posters. He continued the game, ignoring Dana like she wasn't in the room with him.

Dana leaned on his flimsy wooden bookshelf, careful not to let *The Picture of Dorian Gray* topple off. "You know–"

Ace stuck his middle finger up at her long enough to make her more irked than a regular one would and went back to maneuvering the controls.

Dana snatched the electronic away.

"Hey!"

"You let me in," she huffed. "I assumed you wanted to tell me something. Otherwise, you're just wasting my time."

"Then yes," Ace stood up, grabbing his Nintendo back. "Yes, I did want to tell you that the fact you're moving to a different place with your stupid, condescending, utterly pathetic boyfriend is ridiculous because you know I can't afford this apartment on my own." He picked Mango up and thrust her forward. "See? We don't even have enough money to fatten her up. Even the strays lurking around the corner of Arthur's are eating better than she is."

The dog let out a fart.

"Mango needs a diet, my boyfriend is *not* utterly pathetic and I'm not going to break up with him just to cover your ass!"

"I'm not asking you to break up with him, I'm asking you to not move in with him!"

"I'm moving in with him!"

"No, you're not!"

"Yeah, I am. Stop me."

Ace grabbed the roll of duct tape from his nightstand and ripped a piece off.

"Are you serious?" Dana scoffed, grabbing an empty paper towel roll. "Child's play." She whacked his head with it. Ace parried, sticking the tape on her eyebrows.

"You got nothin' on me," he said, shoving her to the ground.

"Freshman fifteen, huh?" Dana squirmed underneath his elbow. The rug's yarn itched her legs. "More like freshman fifty."

"Shut up," Ace groused.

"No wonder you're single."

"No wonder you have a shitty boyfriend."

They wrestled in tiny space, swatting and sissy fighting each other. He aimed a kick at her leg but ended up puncturing through the cheap fabric closet. A hanger fell out, tangling Ace's shirt.

Dana laughed. She started tickling his stomach.

"Stop it!" Ace shrieked, his low, masculine voice a high-pitched bird squawk. "Hey! Stop it! Dee!" He continued to flail around, which only motivated Dana to tickle him more. "Please! DEE!"

Dana collapsed, panting.

Half-read comics and scribble drawings sat in stacks around the small room, testament to their childhood. Childhood, Dana knew, was something Ace was going to have to learn to live without soon. It wouldn't stop him from being the most immature twenty-year-old in the universe, but he would have to transition into a somewhat mature form of adulthood sooner or later.

"Wait here," Dana told him. She headed into the kitchen, weaving through the small dining space in the dark and returned to Ace's bedroom with something in her hands.

"What's that?" He asked.

"Since I'm moving out, it probably means you'll have to as well," Dana unfolded her hands to reveal the ceramic pig-shaped bank that had sat on their kitchen windowsill for three years. "I want you to have this."

Ace stared at Dana in awe. "Wow," he took the trinket and turned it around in his hands gingerly. "This is mom's."

"I know there's nothing in there," Dana said. "Probably like, a penny or something. But it's, you know, a thing." She stretched on the ground, her body snug in between the bed and the wall. "Now that you have a job, you should be pretty good at taking care of yourself."

"It's only for two-ish days."

"But you said it was for a sculpture contest," Dana pointed out. "What if an agent scouts you and you get hired and become insanely rich?"

"Not happening."

"It might."

Ace stood up and fell backward on his bed in the cluttered room. He tossed the clothes hanger away. A few newspaper clippings and unwashed clothes littered the sheets. His eyes were closed.

Dana got up. "Good night, *baby*."

"I'm not a *baby*," Ace muttered. "G'night."

Dana flicked the lights off.

"Good" was irrelevant. At least for tonight.

CHAPTER THREE

MARK
Conclusion of a Divorce: The Day Before

Mark was convinced that every children's health center in the United States of America had at least one fish tank. He eyed the one next to him from underneath his cream-colored fedora. The fish inside it looked blank like they weren't present at the same time and space he was in. Algae clung to the bottom of the glass. A little orange clownfish peeped through the green strands. A stream of bubbles came out the slit of its protruding mouth.

"Ready to go?" Grayson headed towards Mark, a paper cone of distilled water in his hand.

Mark nodded, standing up from the vinyl waiting seat. He arranged his hat.

"How are you?" His friend pushed open the door open to the outside. The outside, where Mark once felt comforted and understood. It didn't make him feel like that anymore, and it wouldn't for a long, long time. About to walk out the clinic, Mark saw her.

Brown to blonde ombré waves. Delicate eye makeup in various shades of orange. A sweet dip in her cupid's bow.

"Oliver? You're up," a man with dark skin and kind eyes called from the nurse's hut, snapping Mark out of it.

His heart rate increased, doing a better *allegro* than what he could play on his keyboard. The woman's back was facing him. A silk dress shirt accentuated her shoulder blades.

"Mark," Grayson waved his hand in front of his unresponsive face. "Mark."

"So, you're not going to say anything," Grayson relaxed the tight knot of his tie as he strolled along the edge of the brick pavement, dangerously close to the road.

Mark was several feet ahead of him. A car screeched past them, causing him to topple, regain his balance, and then walk even faster.

"Stop," Grayson repeated, gripping Mark's arm.

Mark shook him off.

"*Stop.*"

"I couldn't have okay?" Mark barked, turning around just enough he could see Grayson out of the corner of his eye. "I was going to fall into the sewer if I did."

Both of them switched their attention to a set of neon cones barricading an open manhole. They looked at each other. They shared a light chuckle.

"You saw her, didn't you?" Grayson asked, his voice soft. "Even though you didn't really."

The evening sun was descending, the last rays of its blushy glow disappearing. More and more cars drove by, indicating the start of the rush hour. A few pedestrians ambled past them, the ones with briefcases and tired expressions walking in quick strides. Mark plodded away in the direction of the grocery store.

His low-income providing carpenter career did not mean Mark had to eat as well as his job paid him. Frozen TV dinners repelled him, condensed soups had been deemed gag worthy since the mold incident, and those "just add water" powder-into-foods were a solid no. Mark blew open a sealed plastic rectangle to bag the bunch of radishes. He walked further down the produce section, on the lookout for ingredients that could be used in future meals. He was so distracted he didn't even notice the woman standing in front of the bundles of kale until he bumped into her. One of them fell to the ground.

"Oh, I'm so sorry," the woman exclaimed, bending down at the same time with Mark to pick up the greens.

"Yeah, you b–" Mark froze in the middle of his retort.

No. It couldn't be. First the clinic and *then* the supermarket? He had to be hallucinating, but the woman was rigid as well. Her phone had tumbled out of her unzipped purse and into the puddle of water created by the vegetable sprinkler. The impact turned on the device, revealing a long crack on the screen. An email notification from seven minutes ago floated on the lock screen.

Yusuf Bates

SculptFest 2016 Modeling

Dear Ms. Gillan, Congratulations! You have been...

And that was all it took to convince Mark he wasn't dreaming. There, in the flesh, her forehead level with his, was Vanessa Renee Gillan.

"Hi, Mark," Vanessa said, standing up. He had her angelic voice memorized, and it sounded a lot shakier right now.

Was she afraid of him? Mark scrambled to get up while making sure his fedora was secured over his auburn curls and part of his face.

Say hello, his subconscious pressed him. *Don't make a scene, just greet her and move on with it. It's not like you'll ever see her again after tomorrow.* No, he would. He had seen Vanessa everywhere she wouldn't be since the day the grasshoppers and crickets' chirps turned to static.

"He–hel," Mark stuttered. He wanted to run out of there. He wanted to stay and tell her how much he missed her. Or tell her he was better off alone. Anything that wouldn't make him look like a complete idiot who couldn't even get the word "hello" out. But when he peeked out from underneath the brim of his hat, Vanessa was nowhere in sight.

CHAPTER FOUR

FRANK
About November 16, 2008

Eight years ago on a fall afternoon, the front door of the Bates's residency flew open. In thundered Yusuf Bates, his face shining like the headlights of a car in pitch black. A band twinkled on his fourth finger, as bright as the red gold October sun outside.

Like any good friend, Frank had sat him down and poured him a drink to calm his nerves. And like any newly engaged man, Yusuf couldn't get through announcing that he was getting married without giggling like a fool. His future wife was Angie, the woman Yusuf had dated since college and one of Frank's good friends.

Two weeks before the big day, Frank and Jacob, Yusuf's brother, decided to plan a party for him. After all, they couldn't send their best friend off without his last taste of bachelorism. They sat on the shackled roof with two bottles of beer at night, ideas bouncing back and forth. Should they hit their favorite bar joint? Should they stay in or go out? Was it just going to be them or were Yusuf's other friends going to be invited as well?

But sneaking up on the roof was too dangerous–it rained often, which made the shingles slippery, and no plans could be settled with the groom in the house. So one evening, Jacob and Frank went out for a drive. And that's when it happened.

The plush upholstery, soft under his thighs.

Chipped red doors.

65.

Slick. Crunch. Rustle. Pow!

No time to search the whole world around.

Down, down, down.

His ears. His mouth. His lungs.

Those blue, blue veins on pale skin that used to be dark olive.

A week later, thirty-four people's phones lit up with the same email notification at 2:47 p.m. on November 25, 2008. It was a calm Tuesday afternoon, just three days before the wedding.

Dear friends and family,

We have a devastating piece of news. Due to a sudden death in the family, the wedding will be postponed to 1/14/09.

Thank you for understanding,

Yusuf Bates and Angie Saunders

It was never calm again.

•••

FRANK
Two Days Until SculptFest

Sunlight filtered in through the open skylight, illuminating the dust floating in the air. Electric guitar chords crackled out of the working side of the ancient CD player. Frank clenched his hand tighter around his tool. Billie Joe Armstrong's nasal voice reverberated in the large warehouse. Frank tolerated it at first. He smoothed the edges of the moist clay, working like it was any other song playing. But then it got to the chorus.

No time to search the whole world around.

The wooden knife fell out of his grasp with a *thunk.* Frank stood. He pressed the button that popped the disc casket out. He didn't stop there. He lowered the volume despite the fact that there was nothing inside. He turned the stereo off, yanked the plug out from the socket, and was about to take it outside and throw it on the road for a truck to run over before Yusuf interrupted him.

"What are you doing?"

Frank hesitated. "I don't like that song."

"And you're trashing our CD player because of that."

The power cable unraveled from around the player's handle. "No. I just thought I'd, uh," Frank searched for an excuse. "I thought I'd clean it."

Yusuf gave him a strange look. "Alright, man," he nodded in the direction of their project–a collection of three pieces entitled *The Accident, The Disappearance,* and *The Separation.*

Frank didn't smile.

"I would tell you to go ahead and do whatever the heck you feel like doing, but…" Yusuf trailed off when he saw that Frank's facial expression didn't change.

Frank set the black stereo down next to one of the three stalls. His knees crinkled the newspaper bedding as he picked up his blade and returned to shaping the clay again.

Yusuf was right. The one thing he should be focusing on at the moment was SculptFest. It only happened once a year, it targeted sculptors—it was perfect. Anyone who had joined knew it started out as an affair with happy-go-lucky. In the middle of it, that disturbing feeling would catch you, building up to the deadline. It berated him to the point where he was insane. Out of the six years Frank and Yusuf participated, it was always the last few days that had them set to panic and scream mode.

This was what they did for a living. Other than their respective part-time jobs (Frank was a bus driver, Yusuf volunteered three days a week at the clinic in between the two townships), they had zero support. Although SculptFest wasn't well-known or very prestigious in the art world, its grand prize was better than a homeless man getting a free five-course meal. Without the award money, that's who they were going to be if they didn't win this time. Losing last year meant bidding goodbye to their apartment and saying hello to the warehouse.

"Do we still have any of that six-pack left in the fridge?" Yusuf asked, turning around in his swivel chair.

"If you paid any attention," Frank grumbled, wiping his filth-coated hands on the front of his jeans, "we ran out of beer months ago."

Yusuf sighed and returned to his computer. Frank rolled his eyes. He wanted to say it out loud, how unfair it was that Yusuf got to relax and type up emails when he should've started sending them out days ago. Yusuf ate *stale gyros* that the street vendor couldn't sell. The models they were using for their project should've been notified already, and begging for leftover food because they were low on cash was just *pathetic.*

Freeloader, Frank thought.

"I'm sending out the emails, by the way," Yusuf piped up.

Frank ignored him, continuing to work.

"Hey, it's not like I'm not doing anything," Yusuf reasoned, but the sheepish edge to his voice contradicted him.

"Fine," Frank groused.

"Fine," Yusuf mocked him. "That's all you ever do and act and say. I'm fine. Everything is fine. My mood is fine. Blah blah blah," he shut down his computer. "It's a lot easier if you panic out loud."

"I'm not panicking."

"Yes, you are."

Frank glared at the floor. It was true. As much as Frank loved to do what he did, he did not want to live in a wear and tear warehouse for the rest of his life. He wanted to freight train through this last competition and win. He would use his half of the money for a new future. Convincing Yusuf that it was for the better was another situation he could take care of afterward.

"Tell me about the models," Frank said after a brief moment. "You hired them without giving me any background info."

"If you paid any attention," Yusuf continued to tease him, laughing a little at his impression of Frank. "Okay, sorry I hired them without letting you know, but if you—"

"Stop being passive-aggressive. Just say it."

"Okay, okay," Yusuf held his hands up in defense, forcing out more laughter to lighten the solemn mood to no avail. "I'm not being passive-aggressive. They're regulars who go to our exhibit. I hired three—two women and one man."

Frank pried open the dusty lid of a box, sifting through the materials inside. He waited for Yusuf to continue, who realized that Frank was still listening.

"One's a high school student," Yusuf said. "Another is around twenty-years-old. Last one is near our age, I think."

"You know you should've hired them earlier," Frank closed the box in annoyance when he couldn't find anything to use. "We would've been done with the collection by now if you did."

"*We.* You meant *we* should've hired them earlier."

Frank's grip on the cardboard box hardened, his fingernails denting the surface. "No, *you.* All you do is sit there and eat food and ask if there's beer and not do anything. I'm the only person who's actually trying to do a good job."

"Fra—"

Frank wasn't about to let Yusuf win the argument this time. "You said you'd be in charge of this."

"Sorry," Yusuf said, but he didn't sound apologetic at all. He sounded nothing out of his normal sloppy self. "I'm sorry," he repeated, making his teeth go *eee* when he said "sorry" like he was at the dentists'.

"When do you want me to pick them up?" Frank sighed, giving in. There wasn't a point in getting worked up over something that was too late to change.

"Tomorrow at three," Yusuf replied. "The exhibit."

"Done," Frank saved the reminder on his phone and turned it off. He glanced at Yusuf. "Get off your ass," he said in a softer tone, waving him over. "Help me finish this."

The night took no mercy on them, swallowing hours that once felt abundant. In less than forty-eight hours, both of them would be shoved onto a stage before a crowd of five hundred with air to present. Frank shuddered thinking about the scattered applause and the judges' confused expressions.

"It's starting to form," Yusuf insisted when they carved the finishing touches... of a quarter of the sculpture.

Frank stared at their project. It looked like Grandmother Willow from *Pocahontas* tripped over her roots. The thing was jutting out at odd angles, the moist clay was full of lumps, and it was a *masterpiece.* A Play-Doh masterpiece of a five-year-old. Donkey crap.

It was supposed to be the torso of a man.

"Grand plan, huh?" Frank muttered to himself.

Months before today, Yusuf had been elated. He had proposed several plans, which all had sounded good, but then right when Frank thought they were going with one of them at last, the rejections started.

Too hard, Yusuf had complained. *It's boring,* he had whined. *Unoriginal,* he had deemed with a firm nod of his head. And of course, the undefeatable, the all-powerful *no.*

Plan A was to make a marble statue. Frank and Yusuf were more than qualified to exceed their own standards at that. The trend Donatello set was timeless when it came to nude sculptures. Plan B was to create a pair of miniature bronze stallions. It was easy to remove from the mold once it cooled. If they were careful, they could steer clear of last-minute accidents.

But no. No, no, no. Yusuf Bates had to go out of his way to take on the role of the mascot of the stereotypical struggling artist clan and suggest that ooh, maybe they *made a collection of three.* Three sculptures. They barely had enough time for one. Even worse, they were all made out of different materials: clay, Plaster of Paris, and marble.

The last time Frank worked with clay, it was for his art project final in college. He failed. Then he dropped out of Cooper Union to pursue a paycheck so he could stop living off of instant noodles.

Free tuition, his mother had said. *Free tuition, good school, and my son gets expelled.*

Not expelled, momma. Dropped out.

Frank stared at their unfinished sculpture in disappointment. God, it looked like a disas–

A guttural cry interrupted his train of thoughts.

Frank spun around. Yusuf was sprawled out on the thick pine floorboards along with what must have been at least a twenty sheets of paper, each filled with an ocean of text. Three unsealed yellow envelopes were strewn around him. His leg twitched like a rat was biting down on his toes. A blank canvas replaced his kind brown eyes. His mouth was hanging half open, quivering and contorting, trying to scream. The ground protested his weight, filling the room's unsteady silence with a creaking that Frank would never be able to unhear.

Jerk.

Spasm.

Yank.

"Oh my god," Frank whispered in shock, frozen where he was.

Yusuf's torso was uncontainable. A magnet was sucking it forward, lurching it back and forth and back and forth and *everywhere.* A pool of saliva leaked out the corner where his lips met.

Pushing himself to take action, Frank positioned Yusuf onto his side as gingerly as he could. "Please be okay," Frank croaked. He gripped the arm of the couch, losing more breath than Yusuf was.

Thirty seconds disguised as an hour passed. Yusuf's seizure died down, and he regained focus. "Wh-what happened?" He asked, a jigsaw puzzle of incertitude spread across his face.

"You had a seizure," Frank replied. "Are you okay?"

"I'm fine," Yusuf brushed it off like it was no big deal. He stumbled to the couch with Frank's assistance. Half of his body limped on the ground.

"Just take a breather, okay?" Frank said. "Don't move or anything while I clean this mess up." His foot nudged a piece of paper. Yusuf's pupils shrank at the crinkling sound it made. Frank peered at the words on the page. Some of them were written in red. "Do you need water?" Frank asked, returning to Yusuf.

Yusuf nodded. "My cup is down there," he cast his head towards his mug at the foot of the couch. It had been tipped over in the hurry, causing lukewarm coffee to stain the papers around it. Yusuf's hand flinched.

Frank gathered the fallen sheets as Yusuf drank. A sentence on one of them caught his eye.

I want to touch the sun, daddy, it read in a handwriting he recognized. Yusuf's.

Yusuf snatched it away out of nowhere. "It's nothing," he mumbled though Frank didn't question him. "Had to bring some medical documents home from the clinic to file. Diagnosticians like to know everything," he snorted. Yusuf glanced at the page and chuckled. "Usual stuff, ya know? This one's about *strange encounters* a little girl has at night. She's the current talk of the office."

"Oh."

Yusuf folded his shirt sleeve back to check the time on his watch. "I have to go." He grabbed the stack of paper and the envelopes off the coffee table where Frank set it. He shoved it into his worn sling bag in a fluid motion. Making sure his wallet and apartment keys were inside, Yusuf buried everything on his desk inside their drawers.

"Where are you going?" Frank questioned, standing up. "Yusuf, you just had a *seizure*," his eyebrows snapped into anxious caterpillars. "You're not going anywhere."

"Clinic," Yusuf said. He attempted to flatten his wild hair.

"It's eleven at night," Frank protested. "You don't go to work at night."

Yusuf's hand was on the doorknob. "I need to drop this off," he patted his bag.

"The clinic is *closed*," Frank pointed out. He didn't believe what Yusuf was selling.

"If you want dinner, there's a nice gyro place about two miles from here," Yusuf suggested.

"I *know* about the gyro place."

"Fantastic Tzatziki sauce," Yusuf continued absentmindedly. "Homemade Greek yogurt. Tomatoes. The works. And–"

"I want to touch the sun, daddy?"

The door obstructed the moon, causing the reflection in Yusuf's stare to go dark for a second.

"I touch the sun, daddy, doesn't sound like someone's medical history," Frank pressed, endeavoring for Yusuf to tell him more. "What does it mean?"

"Something from the dreams of a five-year-old child who loves to play with Legos and read storybooks featuring piglets. They probably don't mean anything," Yusuf shut Frank's question down with a sneer that was a few steps away from playful.

"I'm worried about you," Frank blurted. "You just had a *seizure*. Can't you just call in and tell them that you'll drop the stuff off the next time you go?"

Yusuf released his hold on the doorknob and looked at Frank in the eye. "I told you I'm fine. Really," he persisted. "You're just being too anxious right now." Yusuf did a little dance move with his feet to prove his point.

A knife poked at Frank's chest. He worried too much for someone whose friend had a near-death experience less than ten minutes ago? "Whatever," he sighed. "Turn off the lights before you—"

Unbothered to close the door, Yusuf headed out. "See you in the morning," his words grew softer. His sneakers rumpled the grass as he walked towards his red pickup truck. Duct tape sealed a crack in the passenger door.

Frank sopped up the spilled coffee with an old T-shirt. Yusuf was hiding something. Something Frank wasn't sure he wanted to know about.

It was well past midnight when Frank laid on his makeshift air mattress bed. The crickets continued to chirp in the dark. *Fwipfwipfwip,* went the overhead fan. The thin blanket twisted in his legs, devoured by his body heat. The CD player sat on the floor across the room, shrouded in darkness where he left it. The moonlight illuminated the metal grid part of the speakers.

No time to search the world around, the lyric echoed in the silence, although the stereo wasn't on. Frank gnawed the inside of his lip. He couldn't believe he used to like that song. It used to be on all the playlists on his iPod, it was the song he listened to after that breakup with Kelly Moore. But then it was played one too many times. It was playing that winter day.

No time to search the whole world around. It was an octave higher this time.

Frank gritted his teeth.

No time to search the whole world around. No time to search the whole world around. No time to search the whole world around.

The same line repeated over and over again, its pitch ascending each time it did like the disc was broken. Frank made a move to unplug the stereo, but then he remembered it wasn't even close to the electrical socket, let alone plugged in.

No time to search the whole world around.

A steady, throbbing overwhelmed him. It pounded in his head. Thundered in his chest. It threw him back eight years to the gelid November evening he killed a man. Someone he knew and loved. He remembered the melting sludge the weather forecasters called snow at breakfast that morning. Driving past the speed limit on the road, car headlights piercing through the cloud of haze in front of them. They were on the way to the giant piece of meadow just a few minutes from Angie's house. He recalled the way Jacob's legs were crossed at the ankle next to him in the passenger seat. The way Jacob's eyes screamed at Frank when his last breath was stolen.

The plush upholstery, soft under his thighs.

Chipped red doors.

65.

Slick. Crunch. Rustle. Pow!

No time to search the whole world around.

Down, down, down.

His ears. His mouth. His lungs.

Those blue, blue veins on pale skin that used to be dark olive.

Maybe it was because he was adjusting the volume on the radio. Maybe it was because the road was slippery. Maybe it was determined by fate that Jacob should die that day. Whatever it was, losing one person had already been enough. Frank didn't want another one to go. But the same question dictated his mind, the same one that he could never finish asking.

What if Yusuf–

The humid June darkness suffocated his entirety. A fine sheen of sweat greased him, heating his body so much the warm air felt cold on his skin.

What if Yusuf–

His brain was being choked. Nausea crawled up the back of his throat. Wasps swarmed him. He could convince himself, he could. Frank told himself that he had been a good friend through those miserable days. He told himself he did everything he could and that Yusuf would get better before anything happened. The excuses grew weaker as they increased.

Oh, honey, the demon brooding inside his head hissed, bitterness laced in its snarl. *God, honey, no. Deceiving yourself isn't going to do any good. Momma's here for you now, don't you worry.* It curled around Frank's neck with satisfaction, the spikes on its tail piercing his skin.

Frank bit down hard.

Who's momma's little murderer?

Blood trickled through his teeth, staining his mouth with a foul, metallic taste.

Are you still doing that routine? The whole, "Ring ring, it's me, Frank. I'm the person who killed you, I had no idea there was cell service six feet deep!" routine?

Frank sat up, trying to calm the vomit burning at the root of his gag reflex.

"You'll be okay," you told Yusuf. "Your wife will forgive you one day and you'll be back to being so in love that you can't see anyone else," you said. Well, his demon doubled back with a peal of laughter. *Wouldn't that be amazing if it happened? Oh, wait. It can't. That's because Clara's gone. And that wouldn't have happened if Jacob died. Who's fault was that?*

Not his. Not his. Not his!

Oh please. Everyone knows it was you.

Barely making it to the bathroom on time, Frank retched into the sink.

You should be more careful with how you execute these murders, his demon continued, merciless. *People are going to find out that you're far from innocent.* It sighed. *It was a cruel thing to do.* Jacob, *Frank. Two weeks before Yusuf's wedding. This is his brother we're talking about here! I know, I know. The crimes villains commit are based on their own agenda. But don't you think you could've waited a little bit longer?*

Frank was not a murderer.

He gagged at the stench, shutting his eyes tight to avoid looking at the putrid mess splashed on the white ceramic.

It was an accident. He couldn't have done anything then.

Just want it to be over, don'tcha? Well, then, go on. Lie. Lie to yourself. Do it. Cover it up and blame it on something else, because really, it's not on you, isn't it?.

A sharp force pierced Frank's chest, vibrating all the way down to the center of his core. He howled. Leftover bits of cheap Chinese takeout clung to the sides of his mouth and stubble. A wet, sticky sensation rolled down his chin.

God, this is a fantastic idea! You have everything you need to construct your perfect lie already! The lake–his demon roared, unable to contain its laughter. *It just had to be there, didn't it? It was practically begging you to*–

Frank splashed cold water on his face. Shaking it off his hands, he looked up to the mirror. He had expected to see himself; the struggling artist, the college dropout, but the person in the glass wasn't him. He was everyone. There were pieces of every person he had ever known glued to his face and together, they formed something dead, something that required a host to live. A machine with no soul.

Low on battery, Frank's flashlight lit the black night outside the warehouse. He stooped next to the hose attached to the side of the house and turned it on. Murky liquid streamed out of the tip, clearing up as it flowed. Frank swung it around with his free hand, watering his bed of indigo hydrangeas.

What if Yusuf kills himself because of me?

Nothing stopped him. There were no voices, no forced reassurance, no self-doubt. The question was raw, sinking into him like bricks on cement. It felt as if he had never considered it before. But he had. He had for eight whole years in secret.

"What if Yusuf kills himself because of me?" entertained a possibility. A road split into several paths, each one leading to a different destination. But there was only one reason that the question existed: Yusuf hated Frank for killing Jacob, regardless if it was on purpose or not. It was a simple explanation, but that was all the ingredients it took to unleash an open season of guilt on Frank.

He went back inside. A glimmer in the corner of his peripheral vision stopped him. The lamp on Yusuf's desk was on, forgotten when he left for the clinic. Right before Frank was about to switch it off, he noticed something. The table wasn't empty anymore. It was occupied by a worn leather notebook; the deep lines embedded in the cover indicating that it held old age. An uncapped pen was blanketed in the pages. Frank flipped it open. Secured with a clip were three photographs of three people.

There was a teenaged girl with toffee-colored hair and piercing gray eyes. An indistinct smile lingered on her face. She looked familiar, but Frank couldn't remember where she was from. In the corner of her picture, Yusuf had marked a number two. Another woman, one who appeared middle-aged, was number three, and a boy wearing a hoodie and a coy smirk was number one.

Frank's finger brushed something–a rounded corner sticking out from underneath the notebook. A furious rush of adrenaline flooded his veins, making him switch his attention to what he touched. An invisible force jerked his hands forward, making them lift the notebook. Three polaroids were there.

Those. Three. Polaroids.

Frank tore his eyes away and began to course through the notebook.

–believing in–

November 16–

I want to touch the sun, daddy.

The impulse that had taken over his body was slain, and Frank pushed the notebook away in silence. His heart was compressed into a shriveled nothing. His eyes were shut tight. The adrenaline in him was replaced with a steady throb of shock. Frank hadn't seen those polaroids in nearly a decade. Yusuf refused to ever look at them again. He even claimed he burned them once. But he hadn't.

They were going to come back, and Frank didn't know if he could stop them this time.

CHAPTER FIVE

FRANK
The Day Before SculptFest

Stripes of sunlight filtered in through the blinds, baking Frank's exposed skin. The digital clock on the shelf read 6:08 a.m. Frank forced himself up, his spine cracking like a chestnut opening. He waddled to the bathroom and cleaned his face. The water had felt like ice burning him last night, but now it was pristine, washing away the wounds. He was hesitant to look into the mirror again. His eyes were dead bloodshot and he had a few pimples, but the machine was gone. In its place was a person. The person who was going to make things right.

Yesterday, Frank found evidence hinting that Yusuf had become unstable again. The last time that happened, Yusuf had attempted to kill himself. Today, Frank was going to fulfill a promise he had made himself a long time ago. July 28 was going to be the last day he spent cleaning up someone else's broken pieces. He had spent far too many years and effort trying to help Yusuf recover from all the disasters he had gone through. He hadn't improved since the day it happened, and Frank couldn't always be there for him. Yet part of him wanted to. Part of him wanted to keep protecting his best friend like a guard dog would. Part of him wanted to stay in the warehouse and wait for his bones to become so fragile that they cracked at the sound of the rain falling through the leak in the roof.

On the other hand, if he left, he could do everything he couldn't do right now. There were no risks to anything he did at the moment. The most he'd lose was an art competition, and that wasn't a big problem as long as they had the means to survive. Leaving put Yusuf's mental state in jeopardy, but it was already something Frank could not save.

Verdict: he couldn't stay. He needed to move out after SculptFest. He couldn't imagine going through each passing day in this place, paving the road to death decades before he was going to be laying in his grave. He craved his life. All he needed now was Yusuf's reassurance.

Undissolved clumps of instant coffee powder molded the bottom of the cup, fighting the flimsy stirrer.

Fact, noun. A thing that was indisputably the case. That's what Google stated. Got upset after your pet dog dropped dead out of the blue? Fact. The dog would not live again no matter how many resurrection spells you bewitched. Pissed off with yourself because your first choice college denied your application? Fact. The school had its reasons not to accept you.

Facts were intangible. Feeling was intangible. If things went wrong, at least Frank wouldn't have to see Yusuf's trust break before his eyes.

He spread open the morning news from another morning, a whiff of ink scenting it. He flicked through the pages like he had every other day. He didn't try to read it. They stopped getting the paper months ago and Frank had memorized each word on every page.

Footsteps approached the front door in unbalanced thuds, a sign of a jaded Yusuf. A series of sharp knocks rattled the door hinges.

"I forgot my key at home," Yusuf groaned outside, his voice raspy like he had been screaming all night.

Frank felt his breath hitch as he cracked it open as wide as the chain lock would allow it. He double checked Yusuf's desk. When he was sure everything was where it was before he found it last night, he let Yusuf in.

Yusuf dropped his satchel on the ground and waddled over to the table, sleep lingering on his steps.

"Where were you last night? You didn't come home."

Wrinkling his nose, Yusuf downed the cup in one gulp. He stuck his tongue out. "Bleh." He commented, stealing a bite of Frank's breakfast bagel. "Thash shtale," Yusuf swallowed, plasticky cheese sticking to the roof of his mouth. "Turned out I had to file some paperwork so I stayed at the office to get it out of the way so we could focus on working." He slumped in his armchair, a throw pillow from a thrift shop hugged tightly against his body. His head was propped up in the palm of his hand. Then he glanced at his table.

Frank's heart lurched forward. Would Yusuf notice that he had gone through his notebook?

Yusuf didn't say anything. The only noise made was his shoes scraping the floor as he moved to put the things on his desk away.

Notebook, left drawer.

Polaroids, right drawer.

Each move Yusuf made made Frank more nervous. It was like his heart was trying to relearn how to beat. If Yusuf said he wouldn't be okay alone, what would Frank do? Then he remembered something else. The photographs of the people inside the notebook.

"What?" Yusuf turned around, alerted by Frank's stare trained on his back.

"Nothing," Frank deflected his question quickly. "We should get to work on the sculptures."

"Yeah," Yusuf agreed.

The pace of Frank's breathing slowed. There was no way Yusuf could have found out what he did last night. There was no way he knew anything about Frank. Then it hit him. Yusuf didn't know.

It unwound like a coil of string in his chest and he could feel it spreading to his fingertips, the dryness of his bones, the warmth of his blood. For nearly a decade, no one knew how much it hurt to be him.

They trudged through another restless two hours. Sculpting tools were scattered around them, an audience to their suffering.

"That's it," Yusuf threw his hands up and stood. He pushed his hair up. "I can't do this anymore. I'm tired."

"Well, so am I," Frank muttered, shaping a curve in the moist clay. "But we can't–"

"–I give up," Yusuf tossed his ink-and-clay-stained rag to his seat. "I don't care."

And just like that, the strings in Frank snapped. One at a time they broke, each ringing out in desperation. He was done bottling up his screams. He was done waiting patiently. He was so damn finished with feeling the need to soften the blow just so it didn't hurt someone who needed to be hurt to learn. "Eight years ago, I killed a man," he blurted, unable to contain himself any longer.

The plush upholstery, soft under his thighs.

"Yes, it was an accident," he forced himself to continue. "Yes, I wish I could go back and make sure it wouldn't have happened. But whether it was intentional or not…"

Chipped red doors.

65.

Slick. Crunch. Rustle. Pow!

"Whether it was an accident or not, whether I could change it or just let it happen, it always stays."

Down, down, down.

"The guilt never goes away," Frank croaked. "Never. Never, never, never, *never!*"

His ears. His mouth. His lungs.

Frank collapsed, his knees slamming on the ground. Splinters dug through the layers of his skin. The skin on his lip peeled, hot and fresh. His head exploded like fire meeting glass.

But he felt nothing.

He laughed out loud, laughed in agony. It was funny, how someone could adapt to doing something, being something, so well over time and find it normal when others couldn't even think of living like they did. "No matter how many times I go to his grave with a sad letter or another apology, it's always there," Frank spat, tears lingering at the rim of his eyes, threatening to spill out. "Always."

Yusuf sat in his chair, pure shock and slight confusion displayed on his face. He leaned forward, about to say something, but Frank didn't give him the chance to.

"And you. Two weeks before your wedding, Yusuf!" Frank shrieked. The space where his ears and jaw connected throbbed, filling his eardrums with white noise. "I ruined the happiest day of your life!" His chest swelled, carrying gratitude, sorrow, torment. "You still forgave me." Frank picked himself up, holding onto the chair next to him for support. His finger shook, pointing at Yusuf. "For so many nights I wondered if it was a lie. That you wanted me to feel at peace because I'm your best friend. I wondered if what I did was going to kill you." His fists wrapped around his hair. His ribcage was on the brink of fracturing. "I could never get to the end of those what if questions. What if Yusuf is lying to me? What if Yusuf hates me?" Frank began to sob. The final string inside him split apart. "What if you kill yourself because of me?"

"Frank, I'd–"

"So? So, Yusuf?" Frank cut him off. "What if? What if you do? God, just hate me, *please!* Hate me for murdering your brother! I am a criminal and I deserve to be punished for my actions so just, so just…" Frank threw himself against the floor over and over again, hungry for a concussion to happen. He wanted to die in this instant. "I want you to feel an overwhelming amount of joy when you watch me bleed," he whimpered, hoarse. "I want you to smile as you stab me one more time. I want you to dance a *fucking Irish jig* on my grave because *I deserve it.*" Frank's heart was pounding to the point where he thought it would rip out of his chest and pump on its own. He messed up. He wasn't supposed to be saying this, saying any of it. He wasn't the one who broke down.

"It's not your fault," Yusuf walked over.

"It is," Frank sputtered.

"No, it's not," Yusuf insisted. "It wasn't your fault and it has never been."

"It might not be my fault, " Frank agreed. The hot summer wind ruffled his shirt. "But do you blame me for it?"

Yusuf opened his mouth, about to answer. No words came out. His expression melted from concerned to ashamed hurt.

"You need–" Frank said, changing the subject. This wasn't about him. "You need help." He regretted saying that. He was not going to fall into this trap again. He wasn't supposed to offer help anymore; he was supposed to take it away.

"Why would I need *help?*" Yusuf was angry now, rubbing his thumbs against his fingers until they flushed pink. "What's the *help* for?"

"You have problems," Frank told him in the most neutral tone he could muster. "I'm going to acknowledge that."

Shut up, Frank.

"Problems?!" Yusuf shrieked. "I don't have problems!"

"If they aren't, they're worth hearing because problems can be solved," Frank countered. He could feel himself start losing control of his words. "I just need to know if you're okay. I need to know if you're going to be okay without me."

Say yes. Say yes.

"Of course I'm okay!" Yusuf yelled, but it felt more like a protest. "Wait, without you? Where are you going?"

"You're not okay," Frank ignored Yusuf's questions. "You don't need to cover it up," he begged. "I'll be–"

Don't say you'll be there for him forever. You won't and you're not going to be.

"I'm not *okay?!*" Yusuf screeched. He was a wild frenzy, spitting and swearing, knocking over things on the coffee table. "I don't need to *cover it up?!* Are you trying to mess with me? Oh," Yusuf bent down to meet Frank's height. He stumbled around, mocking him. "Look, there's Yusuf! Let's screw up his life, goody!" Yusuf iced daggers at Frank.

Frank swallowed. There was one more thing he had to get out. "Last night I couldn't sleep," Frank said. "I went to water the hydrangeas outside and when I came back in, I saw something."

"Saw what?" Yusuf's voice was softer this time. It still had an edge to it, but it was a different kind. The I-know-you-know-I-know-you-know-I-know kind.

"Remember you said you had to go drop those envelopes off at the clinic and you were in a hurry? Well, you didn't turn off the lights so I did right after you left," Frank hesitated. The seed had sprouted vines, wrapping around his limbs.

Yusuf stepped forward, waiting for Frank to continue.

"Well when I came in, the lamp on your desk was on," Yusuf followed Frank's eyes, which were looking at what he was talking about. "So I made a move to turn it off, and I saw what was on your table."

The ball was in Yusuf's court now. "What did you see?" He asked, his tone surprising Frank. It was calm.

"This leather notebook." Frank didn't elaborate on the photos.

Shadows darkened Yusuf's eyes enough for his response contain notes of secrecy. "The majority of that notebook are to-do lists and things I need to buy at the supermarket.

"But I saw–" Frank gulped. He was already waist-deep in this mess, so bringing up the past wouldn't submerge him that much farther anyway. "I saw the words November 16, and something about wanting to touch the sun. That same line was in the documents from yesterday."

A flit of something turbulent swept Yusuf's face for a brief second. "So?"

"I saw the polaroids." There. The bomb had been dropped. He could only wait for the counterattack.

"You mean the ones we used for last year's collage project? Oh, I took them out to draw some inspiration," Yusuf shrugged towards their lump of clay. "That thing's got to look less of a smushed up piece of crap before we present it."

Frank's expectancy plummeted. Yusuf was practically oblivious to everything he had just confessed. Was Frank going insane? Did he dream up what he saw last night? "No, the polaroids were of *them,*" he pressed on.

Yusuf examined him with a set of strange eyes. "I used those for the collage." Oh no. He did *not* just shoot his last piece of evidence down. Frank didn't believe a single word he said, but he let it slip. Once Yusuf left for the clinic again, Frank would activate his plans. "Anyway," Yusuf started to head out again. "I need to go now. Bye."

"One last thing."

"What?"

"Do you blame me?"

"For what?"

"Killing Jacob."

"Fra–"

"*Do you blame me?*" Frank was wrong. Feeling might be intangible, but it could be seen. Yusuf didn't trust his judgment.

Yusuf sucked in his breath and exhaled. His eyelashes touched his dark eye circles once, twice, three times before he opened his mouth and uttered three simple words.

CHAPTER SIX

FRANK
The Day Before SculptFest

"I don't know."

Yusuf was playing it safe. Either he had no guts and was concealing the truth or he was willing to lie to save their friendship. Frank wasn't sure if he wanted to know which one it was.

"You don't know," Frank echoed. Yusuf did, Frank knew it. He just wasn't brave enough to say it out loud. It would've been easier if he had, a bullet shot instead of letting a wound fester. "You. Are. Lying," Frank said each word as if he didn't know the meaning of them put together. "You. Are. Lying?" It came out as a question the second time.

Oh, if Yusuf chose any other situation to play "guardian angel".

Yusuf clawed at the base of his neck, the thumb of his other hand dangling through his belt hoop. Casual, pretending to be off guard when he wasn't.

Frank wished he could leave it at this, knowing Yusuf would be alright if he left. But he needed to bare it all, break the chain of lies. "I couldn't sleep last night," he was shaking on the inside but he spoke in a monotone. Left, right, left. Frank walked over to Yusuf's desk in neat steps. The wooden drawer made a scratching noise against the metal pieces holding it in place as Frank opened it. He took out the notebook.

Yusuf's face froze.

"I was wondering who these people are," he stated in the same robotic voice. He wanted to gauge Yusuf's reaction.

I dare you. I dare you to lie more.

He flipped to the page where the three pictures were. One of them fell out. Yusuf rushed to take it, but Frank was faster. "Who are these people and why are they in this?"

Yusuf's limbs went from slack to attentive. His mouth was an indecisive shape, halfway between a frown and an incredulous gape. "Uh, models," he cleared his throat. "Those are our models."

"Really?" Frank asked.

Yusuf nodded. "See?" He pointed at the photo with the young woman. "That's Alexandra Will." His finger moved over to the other woman. "Vanessa Gillan." Yusuf addressed the third picture, the boy. "Ace Harper."

"But the notes inside," Frank coursed through the paper trying to find the lines that had stood out to him last night. "Look," he directed Yusuf to where it read November 16.

"What about it?" Yusuf asked, confused.

Frank glanced at where he was pointing. *Birthday: November 16,* it read. He checked it again. The words remained the same. Frank blinked, hoping that there had been mucus in his eyes that distracted him. It didn't change. "But that's–but I," he stammered. Yusuf gave him a strange look.

"That's one of the model's birthdays," Yusuf took the notebook out of Frank's fingers gently.

"And–"

"It's a coincidence," Yusuf said without meeting Frank's stare. He put the notebook back into its drawer. He shut it hard.

Frank didn't stop staring.

"Look," Yusuf patted Frank's shoulder. "I'm doing fine these days. You really don't have to worry about me."

"Okay."

"For real. I'm going to be alright."

"Okay."

"Hey," Yusuf gazed into Frank's eyes. The sun made his dark skin glow. "I'm going to miss you."

"Please, no goodbyes yet." Frank picked up his backpack and stuck his metal Thermos into the side pocket, grinning a little. "Thanks for... things. All the things, you know?"

Yusuf shrugged. "It's no biggie."

"I'm going to–" Frank stopped in his tracks, halfway to the exit. The final piece of the puzzle in his head connected to the rest of the picture. How didn't he see it earlier?

Three models. Three polaroids. Three photographs.

"Hey," he pivoted around. "Could I take the models' photos with me? I didn't get a lot of time to look over them so I guess I could uh…"

Yusuf raised an eyebrow.

"I want to go over them during my break before I pick you up," Frank concluded. "If that's okay with you."

"Sure," Yusuf handed the photos to Frank, who stuck them in his jeans pocket.

He was going to drive his usual bus route, pick up passengers, and then during his break, he was going to go to the police station to report three people who were in potential danger.

Sometimes Frank felt like he was a character in a storybook that ended with something worse than a tragic ending–no ending at all. Infinite horror. It would always open with "once upon a time, Yusuf Bates" instead of "once upon a time, Frank Cavallero." He didn't mind being the sidekick. His problem was not being able to save innocent civilians when the hero turned rogue. Now he had his chance. Yusuf had a reputation of being out of whack when he was in one of his "hurricanes", so Frank didn't want to risk any more people getting hurt.

Frank pulled up to the stop in his bus, Bus 59. Eight more stations and he would be on a break. The doors creaked open, a gust of fresh air flowing in to replace the musk of overpowering lavender car freshener and smoke suffocating the interior of the vehicle. A passenger boarded.

"Mark!" Frank exclaimed. A wave of familiarity embraced him.

"Oh," Mark mumbled. "Frank." His unbuttoned plaid shirt was covered in cat fur. His sleeves were rolled up to his elbows, making his arms appear even longer. Mark slumped down in the seat behind Frank. Bags hung under his eyes, hinting at a sleepless night. His head was almost rolling off his neck.

"Haven't seen you in a long time. Nice weather today, eh?" Frank began to ease himself into a conversation, hoping to lose himself while talking for a while. Everyone thought he despised small talk, though the truth was that he enjoyed it pretty much. It gave him a breather from his own problems. "Nice weather today, right?" He said again when Mark remained quiet.

"Mhm," Mark agreed, faint. There was a distant edge to him so Frank didn't prod him anymore.

They picked up more passengers as Frank drove and soon enough, he only had four bus stops until he was done with his route. In the window, Frank saw Mark's reflection. He was hunched over, rubbing his fourth finger. It was naked, sans wedding ring. A hidden clue; one that caused Frank's mind puzzle to deconstruct. There was a new piece. "Wait," Frank's face turned to the color of a sheet of paper. His eyes were unblinking, fixed on the road. All the blood drained from his knuckles when he squeezed the steering wheel. A strong sense of impulse overcame him and he rammed his foot on the gas pedal.

"Whoa!" Mark was thrust forward when the bus lurched, speeding down the lane.

"Slow down!" Another passenger in the back yelled.

Frank switched to the low gear, softening the pressure on the accelerator.

"What was that?" Mark furrowed his brow, his face even redder than before.

"Don't get off the bus," Frank said in a hushed tone, opening the bus doors to let people disembark. A woman glared at him.

"Uhh… it's not my stop yet."

"No," Frank ordered. The piece of the puzzle that wasn't there before clicked into place. "Stay on until the last stop."

God, he hoped it wasn't her. That would break Mark. However, if it was, it would mean that Frank had more support.

"What?" Mark demanded once they reached the bus's final destination.

Frank held out Vanessa Gillan's photo without a word, scared to say anything. He watched Mark's face go through a range of emotions until settling on one: Shock.

"You don't understand," Frank said furiously. He slid the three photos across the counter back to the police investigator. "You need to help me."

"I'm sorry," she replied with a sympathetic smile. "As much as I want to, this case is never going to be approved by my superior."

Frank scoffed. "What, so you're just going to wait to act under the command of someone who earns a better paycheck than you do?" He was worn out. He was *so* tired.

No, he told himself. *You've been fighting long enough. It's time to make it worth it.*

"Wait," the investigator said. Her hands moved from her shirt collar to the desk. "Where did you get this photo?" She held up the picture of the boy wearing the hoodie and a slick haircut.

Frank was tempted to scream. "I got it from my friend," he replied, curling his hands into fists. "He had them in his notebook."

The investigator's relaxed pose stiffened. Her thin lips twitched. She cowered into her uniform, but her expression was fierce.

With a cracking voice, she told Frank the boy in the photograph was her brother.

• • •

MARK
Conclusion of a Divorce: The Big Day

Puh-crack!

Mark's late grandmother's gold-edged china plate broke into five neat fractions right before his eyes. The painted rose clusters stared back at him with an equal amount of aghast. Pringles, Mark's five-year-old ragdoll cat, didn't so much as bristle at the earsplitting sound. Mark's toothbrush fell out of his mouth.

"Shit," he cursed, scrambling around the disarray of used cutlery and turmeric powder from last night's curry.

Wh-bam!

He slipped on saliva and mint toothpaste, smacking his head against the open cabinet. Somehow, the damp towel wrapped around his waist remained there. "Argh," Mark groaned, pushing himself into a sitting position. The glare of the morning sun pierced his eyes, making it hard for him to find his cup. His cat watched him, her big blue doe eyes full of amusement. "Beautiful morning," Mark commented to Pringles, swirling a piece of brioche in his milk until it got soggy. A dark auburn hair (presumably his) floated on the white surface. "Uuugh," Mark fished it out and wiped his hand on his towel. He sat on the kitchen countertop, unshaven legs lodged in the clean side of the sink. His back rested against the cabinet.

11:20 a.m., said the clock in front of him. 11:20.

"Ho, no, no, no, nope." Mark set down his breakfast and got off the table. He flung his way through the laundry until he found a four-day-old plaid dress shirt that smelled decent enough. Fork prongs stabbing the soles of his bare feet, Mark shoved everything within his peripheral vision into his briefcase. He put his fedora on his head, making a mental note to clean the kitchen one day. His back pocket vibrated, causing him to drop everything he was holding. "Ten more minutes and I'll be there," he said before the person on the other end could even start. He hung up. His phone rang again. "Bloody hell, Grayson!" He yelled in panic. "I'm going to be there soon!" The silence before he hung up again told him the caller wasn't Grayson. "What do you want?" Mark asked, lowering his voice a decibel.

"Mr. Sinclair," a woman addressed him. A flicking of paper proceeded. "Your court meeting today was scheduled for 8 o'clock in the morning. It is now 11:21."

"I know." Mark struggled with untangling his shoelaces, "I'll be there soon."

"No, Mr. Sinclair," the woman replied with a tone that was at the bridge between mocking and polite. "No, you will not."

"Well, why not?" He argued. A wisp of smoke danced in front of his eyes. Oh, god, no.

"Our–"

Mark tossed his phone onto the couch without aiming, slid an oven mitt on and threw the oven open. The tart smell of burning blueberries and blackened flour filled the room. Breakfast. Placing the tray on the wet kitchen countertop, Mark pressed a soft kiss to the curve of Pringles's nose. Then he ran outside.

Ssss, said the hot tray in the pool of sink water.

Stuffing a wad of crumpled dollar bills into the taxi driver's hand, Mark sprinted towards the building without waiting to collect his change. His tie still flapped when he reached the front desk. "Mark Sinclair, filing for divorce, I was supposed to be here at eight but I overslept. Tell me where to go," he slammed his hands on the table, spooking the occupied secretary.

"Whoa, man," the secretary widened his eyes and pushed down his brows. "What's your hurry?"

"I'm *late.*"

The man gave him a hard stare before telling Mark to walk down the hall, turn right, and that the judge "ain't happy" with him.

Mark took off, walking in long strides. Running to end the last relationship of his life career was not a wise choice, considering how clumsy he was. He pushed open the door, interrupting a murmurous chatter between the judge and the lawyers. Their heads swiveled to look at him.

"I see you like to take your time," the judge commented, tapping her fingertips on the podium.

"I've been waiting since seven in the morning!" Grayson said in a hushed, angry whisper. "Not a phone call, no notice, *nothing!*"

Mark didn't offer an apology. He just unpacked his briefcase and placed all the documents he would need for the hearing on the wooden table in silence.

Something felt off. He looked around the room. American and state flags? Check. Irritated judge? Check. Then it dawned on him. Vanessa wasn't here. "Why isn't she here?" Mark asked Grayson.

Grayson held back his response for a brief moment before answering. "She left. I persuaded them into waiting for you but I didn't know you'd be this late."

"Well, what's going to happen now?"

With a nonchalant shrug and a sigh, Grayson raised his hand slightly. "Your Honor, my client would like to know, and I quote, what's going to happen now."

The judge clasped her hands together. A wedding band shone on her finger.

The irony, Mark thought.

"Your court time was set at eight AM on July 28, 2016. You were not here on time." She eyed Mark.

He retained fierce eye contact with her.

The judge looked at the clock. It was 11:47. "You are very lucky to have such a good lawyer," she addressed Mark's representative. "Normally, if one of the spouses were not present during a court case like this, we would've proceeded with whoever was there. As I said, since you're lucky to have such a good lawyer, we're going to reschedule your date. But bear in mind that I will only reschedule this hearing once. If you fail to attend, your spouse will be allowed to give her testimony without your presence."

Mark slumped at the bus station. He had had bad mornings, but even tripping face-first in a mound of cow feces at his granddad's farm was better than this.

The woman sitting next to him and pulled out a tube of lipstick that looked like pink cotton candy. She puckered her lips, attempting to apply it without messing up, but a streak still managed to escape past her mouth. It smeared. Mark shuffled down the bench a little. He knew smeared makeup.

"Shit," the woman whispered, using the tip of her finger to wipe it away. Her nails were short, gnawed down to stubbles. They made Mark tenser than he already was. "Excuse me, do you happen to have a tissue?" She turned around to ask him. Her eyes were rich coffee and cream.

"I'll check," Mark replied, his voice soft. He rummaged through his briefcase pocket and pulled out a piece. "Here you go. It's clean," he handed it to the woman. Their fingers touched. Mark flinched, visible enough for her to see.

"Thank you." The woman dabbed the pink stain away.

Bus 59 stopped at the station. Mark boarded in a rush, his head turned 180 degrees and glued onto his neck backward, his eyes fixated on the woman. She scooted further down the bench.

Stumbling over his shoelaces, Mark managed to hand the driver his ticket stub without dropping it twice.

"Mark," a voice belonging to a person who Mark couldn't pinpoint said. It sounded glad. Mark looked up.

"Oh," his face broke into a forced smile. "Frank." Mark hoped he didn't look distressed. He slid into the last available seat, which happened to be at the front, right behind Frank. He groaned internally. He didn't feel like talking to anyone about anything. All he wanted to do was to go home and nap with Pringles.

"Haven't seen you in a long time. Nice weather today, eh?" The engine rumbled back to life, propelling them forward with a harsh lurch.

Mark pretended he couldn't hear Frank speaking.

"Nice weather today, right?" Frank repeated.

Mark chewed on the inside of his lip. There was no escaping now that Frank asked him the same question again. And they were at a red light. "Mhm," he agreed, quiet. Frank seemed to sense that something was a little off with him and stopped trying to make a conversation. A good thing, too. Mark knew he would lash out at some point if Frank continued.

It was a funny thing, getting to know a stranger. They were a void. You could fill them whatever image you wanted them to perceive you as, and they would buy it even if you were wearing a mask. Like an extrovert injected to the brim with life instead of a man with a lack of social skills and a tendency to oversleep. That was who Mark wanted to be around Vanessa. But she saw right through him.

They had met in a peculiar way, in an elevator at the large office space where everyone went to work. Mark had been going up to rent out a small cubicle so he could plan out his new project in peace without having to hear the construction next door. Vanessa had been going down after finishing a therapy session with a child whose father worked at the establishment. No words were exchanged when they got on. They pushed the buttons of their floors before Mark realized that the elevator wasn't going up. Then the lights went out with no warning flicker.

"Hypothetically," Vanessa had said in the dark. "If this elevator were to fall, our best chance of survival would be to lie flat on the ground so the impact gets distributed evenly throughout our bodies, therefore causing minimal damage."

"Well, thanks for telling me that," Mark had snapped back. "Now I'm just going to sit here worrying about the next second and who's going to feed my kitten when I'm dead." That was their first conversation. The elevator returned to functioning after about ten minutes.

Two hours later, Vanessa came back for an emergency session with her patient and crossed paths with Mark again. He remembered feeling embarrassed when he saw her again. Now that they were out of the pitch black, he got a good look at her. He saw her in pieces; the floral decals on her dress, the hem grazing the top of her knees, the neckline meeting just below the hollow in between her collarbones. Wisps of brown to blonde balayage hair that framed her round face and the corners of her coffee-colored eyes. But what he saw as a whole was how she carried herself. Vanessa was a woman of command. She walked like she was going to have afternoon tea with the Queen of England and train an army troop an hour later. If it hadn't been for Mark's uncoordinatedness, they would have remained strangers. With one swift swoosh as they walked past each other in the building's cafe, the next four years of Mark's life started.

Rrrrrip.

Vanessa had gasped, shoving her purse under her armpit to conceal the tear in the side of her dress before Mark could see anything. Her sleeve dangled, revealing a birthmark on her shoulder.

"Hypothetically," Mark had smirked. "That could've been a dress you planned to throw out by the end of the day. But maybe you really like it and have a hard time letting it go, explaining why you're still wearing it now. But judging its state right now, you're probably going to trash it."

"Hypothetically," Vanessa had smiled, each of her pearly whites baring sweet vengeance. "If you weren't a wannabe six-footer with peach fuzz, I would direct you to a kindergarten classroom." She had sniped and sauntered away.

Out of nowhere, the bus swung so hard to the right it jostled Mark to the left, causing him to bang his head on the fingerprint-smudged window. "Whoa!" he winced, rubbing the spot, which was right next to the bruise he earned earlier today. The bus continued to accelerate at a speed even Mark felt uncomfortable at. He saw Frank, who looked like he had just seen a dead person spring out of his grave.

"Slow down!" A passenger yelled from the back. Frank pressed his foot down on the breaks harder.

"What was that?" Mark asked. In that rare moment of complete silence, he heard the most terrifying sound. Frank swallowing. Normally, you're not able to hear someone swallow unless they're drinking something or if you're in close proximity to them. But Mark heard it. Wet saliva sliding down a dry tongue and filling crevices.

"Don't get off the bus," Frank replied.

"Uhh," Mark glanced outside. "It's not my stop yet."

"No," Frank said. The bus rumbled to a stop behind a pickup truck with gas tanks in the back. He turned around to face Mark. His eyes were glazed with something even someone oblivious to emotion could understand. Fear. "Stay on until the last stop."

A box of crayons, three notebooks, and a pencil sharpener had been destroyed within the first ten minutes Mark inhabited his first-grade classroom. He was diagnosed as highly impatient by his parents and teachers. Despite this fact, he promised Frank he wouldn't get off until the final stop.

At least two hours passed before the bus halted at the final destination. "What?" Mark blurted, his anticipation burning to the point where he ached. He had got on the bus at around twelve and now it was almost two in the afternoon.

He saw what was in Frank's hand. It was a photo printed out on paper, little hills made from damp ink on it. A woman with brown and blonde hair stared right back at him. She wore a sleeveless shirt and tight jean leggings. Her shoulder was bare, exposing a pigmented patch about the size of a palm. A birthmark.

Vanessa's birthmark.

CHAPTER SEVEN

YUSUF
One Day Until SculptFest

He waited for the crunch of Frank's footsteps on the dry grass fade into the distance. Fueled, Yusuf sprang into action. He slid open the left drawer of his wooden desk to get his leather notebook. His thumb coursed through the fragile pages in quick strokes to make sure the polaroids and the–

They weren't there. The photos of the models he had hired weren't there. But there was close to no time to lose, and even less to spend worrying about where the photographs had gone. He snatched the thick yellow envelopes lying next to a pile of books he had been meaning to read and stuffed it with his notebook into his bag. With his jaw snapped into a stiff curve, Yusuf left the warehouse in his red pickup truck.

Goodbye, hydrangeas. Goodbye, broken hose.

Hello, Jacob. Hello, Clara. Hello, Angie.

OPEN 24 HRS DAILY

Women's Crew Neck Short Sleeve Classic Tee. Size: M. Color: White. $6.89.

Extra Large Storage Box (Plastic) x1. No lid included. $27.60.

Mrs. Meyer's Clean Day Dish Soap, Lavender, 16 fl oz. $3.49.

THANK YOU FOR SHOPPING WITH US

CHAPTER EIGHT

REID
Summer Vacation: Day Two

Six bangs erupted from the other side of the door.

Knockknockknockknock pause *knockknock.*

Reid knew exactly who the person outside was. He would recognize that pattern anywhere. "I'm going out," he called.

"No, you're not," his mom wiped her oil-coated hands on her apron. Maggie, one of her latest creations, blinked her pixel eyes, a stack of plates secured in her robot claws. Ceramic smithereens dusted the tabletop. "You need to get ready for your interview."

"But mom–"

Alexi pounded on the door again, impatient. It was a wonder that she hadn't broken their front door yet.

"Is that Alexi?" Reid's mom asked in Japanese, snickering.

Reid rolled his eyes.

"She's such a beautiful young lady."

"Hi!" Alexi piped up through the thin space between the door and the wall. "Wait, I heard my name in there, right?"

"Be home *before* six," Reid's mom ordered. "I'm making *yaki saba* tonight, so you better be here for it."

"Okay, okay. Thanks, mom," Reid stuck his phone into the back pocket of his khaki shorts and slipped on his pair blue sunglasses. He took a breath before he unlocked the door, almost hesitant to see Alexi's face.

"Bye, Mrs. Nakamura!"

It was just the two of them now.

She was wearing the same pair of rusted pink tennis sneakers, the ones she had had since like forever. Sunlight bounced off the dips of her wavy hair and shiny eyelids. Alexi had lots of shiny eyelid days.

"Ray Bans, huh?" Alexi commented, her focus dedicated to the baking pavement. Her hands were clasped behind her, still as stone. Like she was holding something.

"Uh, yeah. You gave them to me."

Alexi raised her head. "You… asshole."

"You're the one who's an asshole."

"Donkeys are cute."

"No, they are not."

Alexi smirked until her lips looked like as if she had sucked a lemon. She made her eyeballs look like they were practically popping out of their sockets. She giggled her twinkly giggle.

"I hope you don't do that to the boys at school," Reid said. "'Cuz it sure as hell ain't gon get you a *boo.*"

Alexi pretended to sulk, still laughing. "Who said I liked *boys?*"

"Hah. *Elliot.*"

"For like five minutes!"

Though Alexi was a lot friendlier than yesterday, Reid still tensed up when the glare she gave him flashed through his memory. Even after being friends with Alexi for a fairly long time, whenever they had a spat or a fight or a three-day fall out, he still got nervous when The Wall was put up between them. It was never permanent, but the restraint felt uncomfortable–similar to wearing an itchy wool turtleneck.

"Hey," she said. "Wanna see something?"

"As long as it's not the something you showed me in that day."

Alexi was bouncing on the balls of her feet now, unable to contain her excitement. "And what's that?"

"You know. Fro–"

Splat! A bright yellow-green amphibian leaped onto Reid's shirt, its three-toed feet clinging onto the fabric. Neon eyes with black diamond-shaped slits stared right back.

"Oh, fu–"

Alexi pushed the lock up from Reid's bike and hopped on. "I'll race you to the diner!" She yelled, cycling down the street.

Reid staggered into the diner, panting for air.

"Hey, bean!" Alexi called him over. She slid a plate of overcooked fries with a generous drizzle of Sriracha on them towards him as he sat down on a bar stool.

"Ew, no," Reid took a swig of her iced tea.

"How do you know you don't *like it* if you've never *tried it*?" Alexi coaxed him, tapping a sauce-covered finger on his nose.

"Wow, great, I have another mom now," Reid rolled his eyes. "You're lucky you didn't get that into my nostrils."

Alexi stuck out her tongue. It was bright blue, the tattoo of a raspberry slushie. "Speaking of orifices, don't you think the way hydrogen peroxide does that fizzy thing in your ear feels slightly orgasmic?" She made motions with her hands when she said the adjectives.

"No, you're weird," Reid teased, taking another gulp of Alexi's drink.

"Hey," she whined, grabbing the cup out of his hand. "Mine."

They basked in there, the afternoon streaming in through the windows with specials written on them for a while without saying anything. They took turns with the iced drink, they nibbled on fries. Reid liked this. He liked sitting with her in the diner.

"About yesterday," Alexi piped up, stirring melting tea-flavored ice cubes with the straw. "Sorry about being such a bitch. It's just with all this are we moving or are we not pressure… Things get crazy sometimes."

"Sorry for scraping your ankle with my bike," Reid offered, glancing at the healing skin above Alexi's sock.

"Great," Alexi went back to her normal, peppy self. "Now that we're done with that and can forget about how stupid we were–"

"You were."

"Yeah, yeah, same thing. I have something to tell you." Her storm gray eyes shined. "I got a job!"

Reid laughed out loud.

"I did! I really did!"

"What?" He managed to get out between cackles. "R-Retail?"

Last summer, Alexi worked in retail and had to pay fifty bucks for two shelves she broke and another twenty-five for another one she damaged while working overtime. She claimed she was sentenced to a ban to that store after that.

"Oh my god, you remember," Alexi popped a fry into her mouth. "No, not retail." She swallowed. "Get this," she drummed her thighs for an effect. "Modeling! I'm gonna be a model!"

Reid pretended to examine her like a doctor would. "Not to be rude, but you're five-one. Don't models have to be a certain height?"

Alexi pushed his shoulder lightly. "Well, you're not so tall yourself, Mr. Five-six. And it's not that kind of model."

"Oh really?"

"Gosh, you think I was going to strut down a runway in underwear?" Alexi rolled her eyes. "I wouldn't do that if you paid me. I'm being a model for a sculptor."

"Wow," Reid wiped his hands on the front of his shorts, leaving damp traces of the condensation. "That's cool. Is it like, for a project or something?"

Alexi pushed up her glasses, tucking a strand of her long fringe behind her ear. "Apparently, it's for this competition. It's called SculptFest, I think. I'm actually going to a welcome party thing soon."

"When's soon?" Reid asked, a little disappointed. Spending time with her one on one like this was rare these days. He hated it when she had to go all of a sudden.

"Yikes," Alexi checked the time on her phone. "Soon's now."

"Oh," Reid commented. He tried to think of something to make her stay longer but she was already picking up her backpack.

"So," Alexi shook an ice cube into her mouth and set the plastic cup back on the countertop. She crunched it with gusto, making a funny face to prod a laugh from Reid. It worked. "I'll see you tomorrow, 'kay, bean?"

"'Kay, bean," Reid replied, grinning at her. He extended his hand and they did their quick *slap-slap-bump-bump-fistbump-kapow* handshake. It was hilarious how nice such a childish thing could be sometimes.

"Bye, bean."

The tiny bell attached to the top of the diner's exit tinkled as she stepped back onto the pavement, walking past Reid's bike slotted in the rack.

Reid hoped she wasn't going to move.

• • •

ALEXI
Summer Vacation: Day Two

"Sorry that I'm late!" She shoved the door open.

"No problem," Yusuf smiled. "You're actually right on time."

Someone had clearly tried to make the exhibit look more presentable. A vase of artificial flowers occupied a folding table, along with a tinfoil tray of hors d'oeuvres that looked like they were ordered in bulk. The linoleum floor stuck to the bottom of her rust pink sneakers, moist with a slapdash mop job.

He shook Alexi's hand. "You know me."

"Uh huh," Alexi slid her hand in one fluid motion when his grasp on her lightened.

"This is Vanessa," he introduced her to Flower Woman, who stepped forward with a "hello."

"I'm Ace," College Hottie seized Alexi's hand and shook it firmly.

Alexi didn't know they applied.

"A driver will pick us up in about ten minutes," Yusuf announced. "From there we will be going to a warehouse where we're going to be working on the sculptures."

More trees dotted the side of the road until they were bordered with a thick forest of pine trees and whole beds of fungi. "I had no idea you were engaged in the art industry," Alexi said for the millionth time in audible disbelief.

Frank laughed, turning the steering wheel to make a U-turn. "Bus driving is just my part-time job."

Alexi crossed her legs at the knee. The afternoon sky was darkening with a less leisurely pace than it had before the summer solstice, and soon, an array of golden hues and pink streaks overtook the blue. They turned a sharp left, causing everyone to slant the opposite direction and Alexi to fall smack dab on the ground.

"Sorry about that," Frank apologized, steadying the bus. "Incoming car who was trying to get ahead of us. You guys okay?"

"Yeah, I'm fine," Alexi replied, pushing herself up. She caught a glimpse of Frank's wrist. It was swollen with a bracelet of blisters. Their eyes met in the mirror. In that split second, Frank looked absent. Vacant. In fact, everything about him felt a little off today.

He mouthed something.

"What?" Alexi whispered.

Frank turned his attention back to the road.

They were still driving when Alexi woke up, but everyone else was asleep. "Frank?"

"Yeah?"

"What were you trying to say earlier?"

Frank blinked. Alexi waited.

"If you do not wish to proceed with your application, please close this browser."

"Huh?"

Frank bristled. "I think he wants you to help him keep them alive."

CHAPTER NINE

DANA
Number of Hours Until Packing: Two

Dana sulked at her desk, drained from the piles of work she did today. She didn't want to stay at the office for another minute. The pros of leaving now would be: a) no more cases to ponder over, b) she wouldn't have to talk to any more of her discriminatory coworkers, and c) fewer risks of getting harassed on the walk home.

The cons were: a) her boss's eagle eyes and busybody ears would notice she had gone home two hours before she was allowed to leave, and b) once she got home she'd have to face a horde of cardboard boxes and Mango barking for attention.

She yowled with her head buried in her arms. All Dana wanted to do was to take a cold shower and sleep until four in the afternoon tomorrow.

"Hey *Dana,*" her coworker cackled, and Dana could feel her beady little eyes trained on her back. "Wait, I'm sorry. You don't speak English, do you? Right. Your native tongue is Asian, isn't it?"

Dana remained at her desk.

"Huh," the woman drummed her sharp fingernails on Dana's plastic ID. "Investigator Dana Harper." She traced the barcode. "What an American name for someone who's from China. Mass-produced and cheap."

"Taiwanese. And I was born in Maine. Get it right," Dana lifted up her head and glowered at Satan herself. "And I'm not cheap."

My paycheck has more zeros than all the tests you've ever failed, she thought. *You dense asshole.*

The woman laughed, shooting needles into Dana like she was a pincushion. She swiped Dana's ID card lanyard from her.

"Give it back," Dana glowered, the humid evening heat coloring her cheeks a vibrant shade of tomato.

"Anyone interested in purchasing this young woman?" her coworker waved the piece of plastic around, her sneer broad. A few employees laughed.

"Give it back to me," Dana snapped, standing up. She felt pathetic. She was short in comparison to the tall, svelte woman, and out of comebacks. The entire corner of the office was roaring, twanging each string inside Dana's body.

The woman sneered, and broke her ID card right in the center, letting both halves fall by the wheels of Dana's swivel chair.

"Get out of my office," Dana thundered. "*Now.*"

A hazy LED bulb lit Dana's workspace in the dim room as she trudged through the work she had left. A plastic cup filled with iced water condensed behind the pile of paperwork towering on her desk. Dana threw her pen at the bulletin board in front of her and leaned back, stretching. Her muscles were sore and her eyes stung every time she blinked. Maybe she'd go to the lobby to take a breather. Better yet, she'd see if she could get her card fixed. She headed down to the ground floor. A photograph in the stairwell caught her attention. It was the skank, smiling for the camera as employee of the month. Her hands itched to rip it off the wall and shred it to nothing, but that was a surefire way to get her a pink slip.

"Dana?"

"Hi Bruce," Dana replied halfheartedly.

"Hey," her fellow investigator walked up to her. "I need you to take care of him."

A tall man with an uncertain stance stood behind sliding glass window. He clutched three small paper squares.

• • •

REID
Summer Vacation: Day Two

The evening wind wrapped around him, rippling his sports jersey as he headed towards the police station to conduct his interview. On most days, he had his earbuds with him and an alternative song blasting out of them. Tonight, he ditched them for the sounds of the town he grew up in. Kids fighting over who got the last chicken nugget (a very important argument), excited dogs on walks with their parents, the road preparing for rush hour. But even when a bicycle careened into a pole and its rider fell off, no one helped him up. It disturbed Reid occasionally, how unaware people were here. Right as he was about halfway across the street, a dull gray sedan zoomed through the zebra crossing.

"Sorry!" The driver yelled, his apology covered by the roar of the engines.

"Whoa!" Reid stumbled forwards, almost falling onto the asphalt. "Watch it," he muttered under his breath.

"I don't believe it myself," a familiar Scottish voice sighed.

Reid peeked into one of the offices. His eyes narrowed. It was the reckless driver. He was leaning on a desk belonging to a police officer, his feet crossed at the ankles. Pinched in his long fingers were three paper squares. By the looks of him, it didn't seem like he was sober. His dress shirt was unbuttoned, revealing a white tee stained with something the color of flax. Cat fur coated him, matching the color of his unruly auburn hair.

"But you have to!" The driver raged. Ignoring the man, Reid went into the room next to his, where he was supposed to be instead of spying.

"It's Reid, right?" The policeman flicked through a file with highlighted lines. He shut it close. "How many I help you, young man?"

"Um, hi," Reid said, scouring for his notes inside his backpack. "I was wondering if I could get an interview for–"

"This is my *spouse* we're talking about!" The driver shouted. Despite being next door, he still sounded crystal clear. A *smack* followed. Reid went taut.

"You were saying?" The officer attending to him questioned. He rolled his fingertips on the countertop like there had never been an outburst.

"Oh, I was wondering if I could–"

"No, of course, I don't have the other names! Who the *fuck* do you think I am, a magician? Ooh, look, a bunny!"

The policeman groaned. Reid made few noises of disapproval with him, anxious for the driver to stop being so loud. "*Yes?*" The policeman in front of Reid asked again, annoyed like it was his fault he kept getting cut off and having to repeat himself.

"I need to conduct an interview if that's possible. It's for a summer project."

"Sure," the policeman brightened a little.

"Great, so–" Reid got in before the driver shrieked again.

"Are you kidding me?"

The policeman got out of his swivel chair and poked into the neighboring room. The driver had his fist on a desk, the veins on his forehead bulging so much that one more exclamation he made would cause them to pop out. "Hey mister," Reid's officer warned him. "If you keep shouting, I'm going to have to throw you out of here."

The driver whipped around to face him. "This is outrageous! These three people," he waved the squares, which turned out to be pictures, in front of the policeman's eyes to see, "are about to go missing and no one is doing anything!" He yanked one of the photos and thrust it into Reid's direction to see. "Look! Look at this innocent young lady!"

Reid took a few steps forward to check out who it was. His mouth parted in surprise. Arms quaking like he was about to get a shot, eyes wishing to be mistaken, he looked at the photo again. The "innocent young lady" was Alexi. "I believe you," he found himself saying.

"See?" The driver turned back to the adults. He threw his hands up. "The boy believes me!"

"Yes," Reid continued. He was so confused. "I know her."

"I thought it was a scam, but now I believe you too," the curvaceous policewoman who was sitting behind the desk stood. Her voice was steady, but her expression read otherwise. "Someone came in earlier today and showed me the same pictures. And one of them…" her voice began to trail off weakly. "One of those people is my brother." She stacked the papers in front of her and grabbed a key off of a hook on the wall. "Conference room number three," she said to the driver. "You too," she eyed Reid. "I've got it all settled, Bruce," she addressed Reid's policeman. His mouth was dangling half open.

The lower half of Reid's bare thighs stuck against the plastic chair, sweaty despite the cool air circulating inside the boardroom. The driver tapped his jagged fingernails on the table.

"Water, anyone? Coffee? Tea?" The policewoman poured herself a paper cup of water from the dispenser.

"Jesus, just get on with it," The driver grouched, undoing his tie. He slumped in his seat, crotch straight ahead like he was alone in his own living room.

"Hey," Reid found himself saying again. "Stop being so…" He made a quick hand gesture in the air.

"So what?" The man rolled up the sleeves of his shirt up to his elbows and tossed his cufflinks onto the espresso wooden table.

So dickhead-ish, Reid fumed.

The policewoman smiled at Reid and patted his shoulder. "Why don't we start with introductions?"

"Is being overly optimistic your full-time job?" The driver bared all his teeth in a fake smile. "What are you running here, a kindergarten class?"

"Look," the policewoman replied, dropping the load she took from her office on the desk with a loud thud. "If you have no interest in saving your wife from potential danger like you said she was in, kindly exit the room now. And no," she added when she saw the driver rubberneck after the food, "you may not take any fruit from the fruit basket before you leave. That goes for the granola bars too."

"Ex-wife," the man responded.

"Whatever. I'm not your love consultant. I'm an investigator," the policewoman-who-was-actually-also-an-investigator flared her eyes. "I'm Dana Harper," she said.

It took Reid a moment to remember that she was talking about introductions. "Oh. Hi. I'm Reid," he said.

"Nice to meet you, Reid" Dana beamed. Reid liked her. She had a comforting, matronly tone and her two front teeth were crooked, which made her feel more approachable for some reason. Dana slid Alexi's photo forward. "And how do you know her?"

"School," Reid answered. "We're best friends."

"Before you say something corny like friendship is beautiful, can we move the hell along?" the man took an exaggerated bite of his fruit.

"Shut up, Mark," Dana snapped.

Mark crunched his pear, letting juice and spit coat his mouth.

Reid began to squirm slightly. He didn't care about how awful Mark was, he only cared about how he got ahold of Alexi's picture.

Dana spread the photos across the table, giving each of them the person they knew. "Good. I'm just going to run through some standard investigation questions and then we'll see what we're going to do after that."

"I have a question," Reid piped up.

"Yeah?"

"Why don't we start getting to them right now? I mean, the sooner the better, right?"

"We can't just start driving to someplace, kiddo," Dana's frustration was on the verge of anger. Reid could tell that she had had a long day. "We don't know where to begin. It's a wild goose chase."

"Not if the goose bit you," Reid responded.

Seriously? What a metaphor, wow.

"I think I know where they might be."

"Are you sure your location is right?" Mark fished for a crushed-up piece of paper from his pocket. "Or do you think 15

Amalee Lane in Bronton Township has a, oh, I don't know, higher possibility of being the right place?"

Reid hated Mark so much.

"You go first, Reid," Dana, pretending that Mark was invisible.

"Um, so there's this exhibit near the township high school," Reid mumbled, suddenly meek in the limelight. "My friend goes there a lot. I know how to get there but it's kind of far from here so we'll probably need a car. Or we could take the bus."

Dana stood up and packed all the envelopes and folders into a sling bag. "Let's go. We can take my car. Just give me a second to grab my stuff. Help yourself to the snacks, if you want. I can't guarantee this'll be over fast."

Mark crumpled up his paper and tossed in Dana's way. It hit her shoulder. "I am certainly not going to drive," he announced when she scowled at him. "I call shotgun."

The three acquaintances walked out the police station to Dana's ivy green van. After she had made sure that everyone's seat belt was buckled, she started the ignition and drove according to Reid's instructions to the sculpture exhibit.

Twenty minutes of snarky remarks and childish bickering later, Mark moseyed ahead of them like he was team leader and attempted to push the door of the exhibit open. "It's locked."

"We can see that," Dana rolled her eyes. She pulled a thin metal tool out of her purse.

"Whoa, you can pick a lock?" Reid said in admiration.

"Oh, I wish," Dana laughed, bending to down to work her magic. "This baby does it all by itself. It's a skeleton key," she showed him the implement. "Watching crime movies with my dad and researching on the internet did help me with some other handy tricks, though."

"*Oh ma lord.* Will you quit it with the sentimental gushy-mushy stuff?" Mark whined, snacking on his second pear. His infuriating self leaned casually against the concrete wall, wearing his infuriatingly expensive brogue oxfords, and an infuriatingly cocky smile with infuriatingly straight, white pearls. "You're such a *wuss.*"

"You get off by making other people miserable, I get it." Dana's attention moved from the keyhole to Mark. "Newsflash, Mark Sinclair," she hissed. "I don't know who you are or what you want from me but you sure as hell aren't getting it." Dana pulled the door towards her, pushing down on the handle to slide the lock back so she could open the entrance without making a lot of noise. Together, the three of them crept inside.

Hues of the fading sunset lit the pitch black exhibit. Reid fumbled around for the light switch. The fluorescent bulbs flickered on, revealing a couple of streamers hanging from the windows and a folding table. A tray filled to a third with small appetizers sat on top of it.

Mark hovered near the table, popping cheese and cucumber hors d'oeuvres into his mouth.

"Hey, what's that?" Dana pointed at something enveloped in a white cloth. A cardboard sign saying "do not touch" and "security cameras in operation" was taped onto the metal pole running through the sheet. It looked like a ghost.

Reid disregarded the warning and pinched the hem of the linen, yanking it off. There was a tearing sound when the fabric cut through the pole. A cloud of dust puffed from the sheet as it landed on the ground. Suspended in the middle of the rod were two arteries wrapped in bulging veins, made of detailed glass. A heart. Reid's gaze fell to the base of the sculpture. It was called *untitled,* by an artist whose name he couldn't really distinguish.

"It's beautiful," Mark breathed, joining Reid and Dana. His ice blue eyes shimmered.

"And it might help us," Dana tiptoed closer to the sculpture, plucking a small rectangle wedged in the fine crevice separating the arteries.

"What's that?" Reid asked.

Dana handed him the paper.

If lost, please return to this address:

15 Amalee Lane

Bronton Township, New Jersey

07854

● ● ●

ALEXI
Summer Vacation: Day Two

Alexi awoke to a snug hand shaking her shoulder. "Wake up, sleeping beauty." It was Ace.

They were in the neighboring township, somewhere no one went without good reason. A large wooden warehouse stood outside, framed with overgrown weeds and wildflowers at its base. It wasn't one of those places that could serve as a B&B or hold someone's wedding. It was an old building. So old that Alexi knew the wood would have a dense touch to it caused by all the rain from over the years. A trickle of water leaked out a loosely coiled garden house. Split wall boards were beside it, leaving an entrance wide enough to fit a couple of rats. Alexi's skin prickled at the thought of rodents scurrying around in the shadows. This wasn't even a place someone could live in, let alone go inside. Her stomach shrank.

Dum. Dum. Dum, said her heart.

"I need to close the doors," Frank said from behind her, waiting for Alexi to get off the bus.

Maybe they were stopping for a water break.

"We're here?"

Frank studied the warehouse with an expression that was foreign to Alexi–a cross between weary and restless.

"We're here."

The interior was a tornado. Paint cards were pinned across the entire surface of one side of the wall. Shards of clay were scattered on the pinewood floorboards. A mysterious powder substance coated the furniture, which looked just as exhausted as the outside. Twin desks stood in one corner, with a plastic board at the foot of them acting as a bulletin board. Three rooms that couldn't be larger than closets were in the back. Two air mattresses occupied the space next to it. "Welcome to our workshop!" Yusuf announced with a tight smile.

Vanessa was perched on top of a wanton milk crate, compacting herself as much as she could to avoid the dirt on the ground.

"Sorry about the mess," Yusuf added, waving his hand around at the filth.

Ace kicked an empty beer bottle out of his way.

Alexi felt uneasy. She wasn't prepared for any of this. She had been expecting a clean room with abundant art materials and cameras and a project, not a warehouse with a few paintbrushes and a giant lump of clay in the center of the room.

"As you can see," Yusuf let out a laugh that sounded fake, "we're not making a lot of progress, which is why we hired you. We just need you for some measurements, modeling, and whatever else might come up."

Alexi didn't want to know what else could come up.

"Frank will drive you back to the exhibit tomorrow at eight in the morning," Yusuf nodded at the bus driver. "You're also very welcome to stay and attend the festival which we will be presenting our project at." The muscle beneath his left eye was twitching. The speed Yusuf was rubbing his thumb against his index finger intensified. He was nervous, Alexi observed. Why was he nervous?

"Hey," Ace held up a minuscule model of a car made from metal. Alexi peered at it. There were numbers carved into the roof: 11/16/08. "This is so cool."

"I didn't make that," Yusuf's relaxed shoulders went rigid. He didn't look at Ace. "Frank did," he added, softer.

Tck. Tcktck. Tck, the tree branch tapped on the skylight, impatient like it was waiting for something.

"Close the browser," a hoarse voice whispered. Alexi turned her attention from Yusuf to the origin of the sound. It was Frank, hanging around in the corner of the room. He was ripping up a strip of paper in his hands. Alexi looked closer. It was a receipt. "Close the browser," he murmured again.

"Frank, you good?" Yusuf asked, breaking Frank's spell.

He blinked as if emerging from a long sleep. "Yes."

Yusuf cleared his throat, redirecting everyone's focus back to him. "There are three stalls in this warehouse," he nodded at each one on his right side. "Please take the paper bag with your initials on it and head into a stall and await my further instructions. After that, I'm going to bring you into the studio," he patted a door Alexi hadn't noticed upon entering, "and take some photos to use. Then Frank and I are going to start working on them. That's when you're going to come in real handy."

A glaze covered Frank's eyes when Yusuf said they were going to "come in real handy". He didn't look alive.

That's when Alexi decided to do something. "Sorry to interrupt," she reached into her messenger bag for her phone. "I just need to make a quick phone call outside." Without waiting for a response, Alexi bolted out of there.

Her mom picked up on the second ring.

"Okay mom," Alexi started before her mother could greet her. "Don't freak out but I think the man who hired me for a job is acting really weird. And the cell service signal is really weak so whatever you're gonna say has gotta be quick."

"What do you mean by weird?" Her mom replied, with her feet going *tap-tap-tap* and her jaw squeezed together.

"Is that Lex?" Alexi heard her little brother ask.

"He didn't say it was an overnight job on the application form," Alexi explained. "He just told us that we're only getting back to the exhibit tomorrow morning at eight in the morning. Also, the place we're at is really old. Like ancient. It feels weird."

"What?!"

Oops.

Ears ringing, Alexi winced.

"I am coming to pick you up right now," her mom huffed in short breaths. "You said that this was a joint partnership with school thing, not an actual job. God, I cannot believe I let you slip right out the door like that. Where are you?"

Alexi began to think that calling was a bad idea. She could already hear the lecture she was going to get in the car on how her safety was "something you should be more responsible about" and how she would be "grounded for two weeks, young lady". "Mom, I'm fine, I just–"

"*Alexandra Will.*"

Alexi's toes curled in her sweaty socks. This was just the worst. "I don't know?"

"You really don't know or you don't want to tell me?"

"I really don't know." Alexi was practically shoving her head into her neck, waiting for her mother to scream. But she didn't.

"Do you think you'll be okay until the morning? I don't–"

The tiny bar on the top of her phone drained before Alexi could answer. Then the fuzz on the back of her neck electrified. Then the forest started to scream at her, the sky got sucked into a whirlpool of more colors than she could see, the air collided, leaving her overflown with oxygen in one moment and gasping for it the next. Then she sensed another heartbeat. Rugged breaths. The scent of smoke and acrylic paints.

"Hello."

Dum. Dum. Dum, went her pulse.

Tck. Tcktck. Tck, went the tree branch whispering against the window.

"I didn't mean to spook you," Yusuf had chuckled. There was a drop in his voice. An undertone Alexi didn't like. "Why don't you come in first?" he had suggested with his warm grin and his warm eyes.

"I–"

"Alexi!" Frank had yelled from the entrance of the warehouse. He waved. "We're waiting for you." Reluctantly, Alexi had agreed to return back inside.

No harm in that, she had convinced herself. *It's safer than waiting on the side of the road in the middle of nowhere. I'm just being too uptight, and no one likes an uptight person.*

Alexi was in one of the three rooms, a kerosene lamp feeding it dim lighting. The partitions, loose shafts of pine, were bare except for some clumsily glued hooks. There was also a chair. It was tiny, fit for a child. A coat of paint covered it–bright yellow which deepened into a tangerine so vivid Alexi could taste it. And like everything else in the warehouse, it was old.

"Open your bags," Yusuf instructed. "You should have a set of clothes, and maybe some accessories in them. Please wear them."

Alexi tore the paper apart. Out fell a neatly folded pile of clothing. But something had made the impact sound heavier. She flattened each item.

There, in a bed of paisley pattern, was a necklace with a pendant engraved with the letter C. The metal was singed around the corners. Necklaces were golden and silver and treasured. From a loved one. Not like this one; a damaged trinket that looked like it had been crafted with poison.

What does it mean? Alexi wondered. She ran her thumb over the silver delicately, feeling for nonexistent clues.

"Where's Frank?" Ace asked in the stall to her left.

Alexi realized she was wondering the same thing. The last she had seen Frank was when he was beckoning her back into the warehouse. After that, he was gone. The only people here were Vanessa and Ace in their respective cubicles. And Yusuf.

Vibrant, peacock blue smeared on a wooden surface, Alexi remembered. Not on the table. Not on the chair. Not on the ground. On the wall. A single streak of paint did not belong on the wall. "Frank?" She called.

"Frank's right here," Yusuf answered.

"Hi," Frank assured them.

Alexi pulled on the shirt. She was just being paranoid. The lamp on the flower decals cast red and gold shadows on the plywood floor.

A new sound added to the *dum-dum-dums* and the *tck-tcktck-tcks.*

Shhk... Shhk... Shhk, shuffling footsteps echoed.

"When you're ready, you can come out," Yusuf said.

Alexi hesitated before opening the door. Yusuf and Frank were standing near the coffee table. Yusuf looked cheerful. Frank still looked absent. She chewed the soft muscle coating the inside of her cheek.

"I'm going to go get something," Yusuf told the three of the models.

"Close the browser," Frank's hollow voice whimpered, irking Alexi. It was barely audible and his face was stretched wide with a strained grin, but she heard him. What the hell was he talking about? There was no browser. And even if there were, why would anyone need to close it?

But what really spooked Alexi was that Frank didn't sound like what he had before. Everything he had said since the moment Alexi met him all sounded like warnings. Red flags. Now it was a cry for help.

"Ace," Yusuf called, breaking Alexi's train of thoughts. "Ready?"

"–And that's how that poor little hamster died," Frank shook his head, laughing. "But that's not the end of the story."

"I'll be waiting to hear you finish it," Ace replied, standing up from his seat. "Let's go." They were all crowded around the table, talking without her. Alexi felt lost.

"Hey," Frank cast a glance in her direction. "You okay?" Before Alexi could say anything, a door opened, its groan coming from the left.

"Jacob."

Click.

"How are you still alive?"

CHAPTER TEN

REID
Summer Vacation: Days Two and Three

According to Reid's mental log, this was what happened in the past two hours:

Mark ate four pears, two granola bars, and half a pack of gum.

Dana honked the car horn twelve times and yelled twenty-three obscenities, most of them made up, like "chicken-throated son of a gun" and "banana slug dumbass driver".

Reid wanted to sleep but couldn't fall asleep because he was thinking about falling asleep so much it kept him awake.

The highway was lit up with the traffic jam, an endless snake of red and white lights down the road. 15 Amalee Lane was still out of reach. They weren't even out of their own township due to how packed it was.

"You do realize that we're only doing this because there's a slim chance these people are in danger, right?" Mark said.

"A slim chance is better than no chance," Dana replied.

"We don't really have anything to go on," Reid shrugged from the backseat. "Except for those pictures. Hey Mark, where'd you get them?"

"This bus driver I've known for quite some time."

Reid let that register. Today was so weird.

"Dana," Mark twirled a pear core by its stem. He was sitting in the shotgun seat. "Dana, Dana, Dana."

"What?" Dana tucked a strand of her black hair behind her ear, revealing a leaf-shaped cartilage piercing.

"Nothing."

Reid poked his head in between the two front seats, careful not to knock the styrofoam cups out of their holders. "Are we there yet?" He asked in the most innocent voice he could muster. He was fully aware how annoying he sounded, but as a mild claustrophobic stuck in a compacted sedan for an extended period of time, he had at least a small right to be a pest.

"Why don't you take a nap?" Dana suggested, sighing.

"I can't fall asleep."

"Say," Mark piped up, unwrapping a chocolate nut bar. He sunk his teeth into it and chewed like a llama, which seemed to spark Dana's fuse. Her grip on the steering wheel tightened, making her knuckles white. "Are you sure we're on the right route?"

Dana slammed her palm on the car horn, making Reid jolt back in surprise. A few cars beeped back at them. "Sweet mother of

Jesus, Mark Middle Name Sinclair!" She screeched, giving Mark a death glare.

"Andrew."

At a glance, Dana was a sweet and gentle woman who took care of you like a mother would. But when she was mad, damn could she fire up.

For a while, all three of them were filled with a the no-words-left-to-say silence. Then Mark turned on the radio. He switched from static station to station until he got to one playing a song. "Think of the tender things we were working on," he started to sing quietly. He was a good singer. He didn't have Italian opera singer vocals, but his voice was deep and smooth like bathwater with the temperature just right.

By the time the song got to the chorus, all of them were belting the lyrics while the post-rush hour dissolved.

On a second thought, *Don't You (Forget About Me)* had never sounded so eery.

Six rounds of Twenty Questions later, they were off the turnpike and on a road with no other cars. "I can't drive anymore," Mark groaned. He and Dana had switched shifts when she couldn't keep on going, but Mark wasn't holding up so well either.

"What a wimp," Dana muttered under her breath. But with Mark's fedora draped over her face, she didn't look like she could get behind the wheel either.

"I don't even have my learner's permit yet," Reid mumbled from the back, spread across the entire line of seats like a human earthworm.

"There's a motel over there," Mark said. "And we're heading into a forest so I think it's best if we stop for the night."

"Stop?" Reid popped up so quickly the insides of his head swirled, making him lightheaded. He held onto the leather seat while trying not to hurl. "We can't stop," he burped, releasing the gross feeling. "'Scuse me."

Dana snored.

"We have to," Mark replied in a hushed tone, turning off the ignition. He tried to wake Dana up, but she was as motionless as a log. He got out of the car.

"But Alexi," Reid protested, remembering why they were here. "Ace. *Vanessa.*"

But Mark already had Dana on his back, piggyback-style, ambling towards the flickering neon sign that read *Bronton Motel,* and *CABLE TV FREE WIFI CONTINENTAL BREAKFAST* underneath it.

Reid had no choice but to follow.

The only word to describe the room was dingy.

It's our last available room, the front desk had confirmed.

There was one twin-sized bed with a questionable blanket, a funky orange armchair with a spring threatening to poke out through the polyester, and the mini fridge (if you could call it that) contained a paper bag that held something Reid could smell with the door closed. Dana was lying on the bed with Mark's plaid shirt spread underneath her.

"You don't understand," Reid tried to reason with the man, who stared out the window at the night.

"I do. You need to get to your friend. I get it. But there's no way you can do that at this hour without a car."

"Yes, I can," Reid hissed, clenching his fists. "I can run right out that door and I'll keep running until I find her."

"Reid," Dana rolled over, drowsiness slurring her speech. "It's dangerous."

So is being a feminist in the twenty-first century. And drinking underage. And about a million other things.

"You don't control me," Reid argued. "You're not my parents."

My parents, he remembered. *Oh god, dad's going to have to dig me up from my grave if he wants to kill me again after mom does.*

"Yes, we can," Mark said, sat on the edge of the bed, running a hand through his coarse hair. "We're your temporary guardians so you're going to have to listen to us for now, lad."

"Reid," Dana pleaded, standing up. She plodded over to Reid and wiped a wanton fleck of dirt from his cheek. "It's not safe to go out there alone."

"I'm sixteen. I'll do whatever the hell I want to. And no, you're not my temporary guardians."

Dana slumped into the old armchair, careful to avoid the area of the spring. She looked incredibly jaded.

"So can I go?"

"I thought you said you were sixteen and could do whatever the hell you wanted to," Dana mumbled. "We're not your guardians anyway. We're strangers."

A little shock of worry filtered through Reid. Throughout the start of the trip, he had to constantly remind himself that these two people, although nice most of the time, were people he had known for less than a day. Over time, he began to forget that. They could be conspiring to kill him, for all he knew. But they didn't seem like bad people. They weren't like most adults, condescending and oblivious to his opinions. Even Mark was alright sometimes. Of course, that was the perfect disguise for two conspiring murderers.

"Go get some sleep," Mark muttered, his eyelids drawn over his weary blue eyes. "We'll be on the road before you know it."

"Turn off the lights, please," Dana added. "Goodnight, sweetheart."

"Goodnight," Reid replied. He flicked off the switch that perished the glow emitting from the lightbulb.

Reid sat on the closed lid of the toilet. He had been swallowed whole by total darkness for a solid hour already, and he couldn't see much given that the single light source were faint traces of moonlight slithering in through the window. The stench of the bathroom almost made him give up all the fruit and nutrition bars he had during the trip. There were tiles for floors and tiles for walls, and they were all caked in mystery dirt.

He turned on his phone. He turned it off. Alexi still hadn't responded to his message. That had to be a sign she was in trouble... Right?

His butt cheeks were getting numb from sitting for so long without moving. Reid groped around for the doorknob. Pressing the door down as hard as he could so it wouldn't make noise when he opened it, he turned the knob slowly. He crept to the main room. They were both sleeping–Mark with a little drool trailing out of the side of his mouth and Dana curled up into a fetus position, snoring.

He headed towards the armchair that Mark was slumped in to get his backpack. Holding his breath, Reid used his fingers to pry the strap out from underneath red curls.

"*Snork!*" Dana's nose interjected from behind him, causing Reid to accidentally tug a strand of Mark's hair instead of his backpack.

Oh no, he thought as Mark began to shift around. He crouched down, his heart pounding. It felt like forever until Mark stilled, allowing Reid get his bag without disturbing his beauty sleep. He went back into the bathroom to get the first aid kit. Right as he was about to open the cabinet, a gust of hot air gushed in through the small window, slamming the door shut with a sound *bang!*. Reid sprang into action. He tore open the kit, grabbing whatever was within reach.

"Hey, did you–" The rest of Mark's sentence was drowned out by the beating of Reid's heart moving from his chest to his ears. He rushed towards the exit, his hand stretched towards out to grasp the doorknob–

He fell. The impact sent a shock of pain throughout his whole leg. One of the tiles that weren't stuck all the way to the ground lacerated his knee and Reid felt a pool of warmth flower out from his skin.

"Reid?" Mark called. "Is that you?"

Reid bolted out of the bathroom. Out of the room. Out of the motel.

With the crescent moon running with him behind tall pine trees, Reid ran. His thigh muscles burned as they lunged. The deafening beating of his heart slammed into his ears every time it pumped.

I'm going to get to you, his feet propelled him forward. He sprinted even faster at the thought of seeing her again. To be able to race bicycles with her, eat cheeseburgers (extra pickles and no tomatoes on her's, no pickles and extra tomatoes on his) at the diner with her, participating in their embarrassing bi-weekly lip sync battles.

But if he didn't get there on time… She would be gone.

So he charged. He charged for her life, to fulfill the want of being with her. He wanted to hear her point and squeal, "cows!" when they passed them while on a long walk, he wanted to doze off in the middle their late-night video calls, he wanted to feel her fingers digging into his hand when they arm wrestled. Hell, he'd do anything just to help her with her AP bio homework.

They were broken parts of something magical without each other.

CHAPTER ELEVEN

YUSUF
The Accident

He lugged the plastic container of water in through the back door of the studio and set in the center of the green screen-covered floor. Yusuf stuck his head out to check on what Frank and the models were doing. Telling that hamster story was Frank's choice of icebreaker, apparently. "Ace," Yusuf called. "Ready?"

"–And that's how that poor little hamster died," Frank shook his head, laughing. "But that's not the end of the story."

"I'll be waiting to hear you finish it," Ace chuckled, standing up from his seat. He walked towards Yusuf. "Let's go." His jet black eyes smiled, and for a split second, they almost looked cognac. They held Yusuf's reflection in them.

If Frank said something, Yusuf didn't hear it. "Jacob," Yusuf found himself saying. "How are you still alive?"

A welcoming smile and a pair of twin dimples beamed at him. "I never went anywhere," Memory-Jacob replied. Then his form flickered, turning back into Ace.

"What?" The young man asked him, confused.

Yusuf tried not to pay attention to Ace's face and not let his stare wander to his torso, which was donning Jacob's old shirt. "Oh," he said. He blinked. "I'm sorry, I was just mumbling to myself there." He pushed the door open wider to let Ace inside.

"What's that water tank doing there?" Ace pointed to the large container sitting on the green screen half of the room.

"I'll get to that in one second," Yusuf replied, heading over to his station where his equipment was. "Let me just set this up real quick and we can start, okay? I won't take long." His hands fumbled to turn the camera on while he made himself comfortable on the short wooden stool behind it. All of a sudden, the device closed in on Ace's eyes.

No, Yusuf pleaded when they began to lighten. They were amber again, orbs of infinite universe. *Jacob, please. Not right now.* But his inner desires fought, and they fought hard. His conscious split into half.

In one world, he was taking measurements in his head, running through a list of materials he could use for the sculpture. In another, he didn't exist in this current time and space. He was in the winter of 2008, at his parents' house with Jacob, knowing exactly what was going to happen next. In both dimensions, Yusuf wanted something more than a new apartment or winning SculptFest: he wanted Jacob to be alive.

"Uh, hello?"

Yusuf snapped out of his trance. He zoomed out on the camera. "Sorry," he laughed a little, attempting to appear like nothing was wrong. "This camera is so old. Takes forever to get the angles right." He grabbed the box of soap on the table beside him.

"Soap?" Ace asked when Yusuf took the white rectangle out of its smushed cardboard packaging, swooshing it around in the tank. He didn't stop until the water was misty with bubbles and suds.

"You'll see," Yusuf went back to where the table was and took one of the three yellow envelopes marked "The Accident" and undid the small metal hook that kept it secured. "So, the sculpture you will be modeling for is called *The Accident.* You'll be depicting a drowning man." Yusuf scanned the handwritten papers–his diary. "I'm going to be focusing on the area of your torso, specifically how it looks when you're submerged in water. That's what the container's for. Still water doesn't really have much to it so I added the soap to create a little texture." Yusuf didn't tell Ace he added the soap because he had his first panic attack in a bathtub after Jacob's death.

"Okay," Ace replied. "Cool." He placed one leg into the water tank. "Ooh," he lit up, sinking his whole body into the water. "This feels good."

Yusuf forced out laughter despite feeling his chest starting to close up. "Yes, I guess it does. Could you twist your body to the right while you sit with your knees bent slightly up?"

"Like this?"

"Yes, that's it," Yusuf said, his index finger hovering above the button that activated the shutter. He snapped the photograph.

It was a good photo. The sunlight was hitting the young man where Yusuf needed it to, the creases on the thin cotton shirt were how he envisioned them: defined but with a fluid appearance. Like something an angel would wear.

Maybe that's what Jacob's shirt looked like when he was dying. The thought was unasked for. Interruptive.

Yusuf's hand went slack, holding down the shutter release. Blinding light stammered out from the top of the camera in rapid flashes.

"Is everything okay there?" Ace leaned against the makeshift tub with his arms crossed on the edge. He was squinting.

Yusuf couldn't form an answer. A switch in his head turned on, lighting up all the nooks and crannies of the dead place. He searched through the cabinets of his thoughts, skimmed through files until he saw it: Jacob's yellow raincoat hanging on the hook next to the front door. A travel pack of tissues was stuck in one of the pockets. The hem's string was unraveling.

"You told me after lunch that late winter afternoon," Yusuf murmured. "That you were going out with Frank that evening for a drive. You were stifling your laughter as you said it, trying to hide the fact that the reason you were heading out later that night was to plan my bachelor party."

Plink. Plinkplink. Plinkplinkplink.

Rain hit the ground, squeezing through the cracks. A sliver of grass sprouted through and the floor expanded into a field. The walls of the stall crumbled to dust. Smooth kitchen tiles ran underneath Yusuf's feet, spreading over the green. Furniture began constructing itself around him: the pebbled sink, the copper measuring cups tucking themselves away inside drawers, the plate of leftover food with a layer of saran wrap covering it. After a brief moment, it settled down, locking into place.

"Hey, Yus," Memory-Jacob greeted him, entering the kitchen and beelining to the cabinet to rummage for a snack.

"Hi," Yusuf replied, stirring his mug of hot chocolate in his hands. He held his breath so he wouldn't vomit at the revolting smell. That was the thing about trauma–it ruins everything you have at a moment.

"Frank and I are taking the car for a spin later," he announced, ripping open a bag of banana chips. His favorite. "Wanna come?" Memory-Jacob giggled through a mouthful. "We're–"

"Watching the sunset," Memory-Frank appeared next to him, clapping a hand on Memory-Jacob's shoulder. He winked at Yusuf, clicking his tongue. Yusuf grinned. Those two could never keep a secret.

But when he saw the time on the clock, he stiffened. The second hand on the clock was ticking way too quickly now. He was running out of time.

Do something, you idiot! His brain screamed at him.

"I'm going to go start the car," Memory-Frank told Memory-Jacob, leaving the room.

"No!" Yusuf shouted without thinking.

Memory-Frank paused, his hand brushing the wall. His mouth asked Yusuf what was wrong, but that pair of eyes could never fool him. They whispered to Yusuf that it was too late to change anything.

No, he thought, determined. *I'm going to save Jacob.*

You know he's not real, a voice said in his head. *I know you can see him over there by the counter with his banana chips, but he's not. This a hallucination.* It hesitated, about to deliver the words that he had spent his whole life trying to change. *Yusuf... Jacob is dead.*

Memory-Jacob held out the bag of snacks in Yusuf's direction. Yusuf shook his head and his brother returned to scarfing down the chips.

"You coming?" Memory-Frank shouted over the roar of the engine. Memory-Jacob grabbed his yellow raincoat from the hook pinned near the front door. The pack of tissues fell out. Yusuf chased after him, about to grab him.

"Jac–" His fingers closed around the back of Memory-Jacob's shirt collar, but there was nothing.

"What?" His brother turned around.

"N-nothing," Yusuf stuttered. His heartbeat thumped in a broken beat, syncing with his heavy breaths.

"Okay, then," Memory-Jacob shrugged the hood of his raincoat on and raced out the door.

"D-Don't go," Yusuf choked out, watching him leave, watching him get into the vehicle. He sank to the ground, his knees cushioned by the thick rug.

"I gotta," Memory-Jacob said, his voice loud and clear despite the red exterior of the car moving out of Yusuf's line of sight.

His surroundings vanished again, replaced by the cream-white walls of the bathroom, where Yusuf was after he learned Jacob had passed. The water was cold. Ice cold, with suds in it. It seeped in through the layers of Yusuf's skin, filling him up to his chest with liquid. The still water rippled. His first panic attack.

He was drowning now, sinking into the bathtub slowly. The more gradual it became, the more he panicked. His limbs froze, numb to the bone. He was frozen there, his chin grazing the surface.

Screeching wheels.

Shrieks for help.

Thrashing limbs.

"Help," Yusuf gasped, right before a long ribbon leaped up, spewing slime everywhere. It was an eel, with the scales of a fish. It began cramming itself into his mouth against his will, plunging down his throat before he could even gag. Shards of its skin pierced into the walls of his flesh. Each individual flake was consuming him alive. He could feel the creature's every movement. It slithered even further, exiting his stomach and into his intestines. The last of its tail glided inside. "Help," Yusuf tried again, but no voice came out. "Help. Help!" Each cry dissipated into the air as a soundless distress signal. "Hel–" Something yanked him underwater.

Without his noticing, a whole swarm of the eels had intertwined his body. They had tentacles too, leaving purple blotches on his skin where they had latched on like leeches. The tub was an endless sea. They dragged him to the bottom, towards the drain.

I'm going to die, he thought, giving up on fighting for air. The eels loosened, swimming away. Yusuf was fading now. The passing seconds invited the silk of the water to embrace him, kill him gently. A second before Yusuf blacked out, he heard Jacob.

"Goodbye, Yusuf."

His eyelids fluttered open when he heard a series of splashing noises. The camera was no longer strung around his neck. He wasn't positioned on the ground anymore. Yusuf was in the tank, soaked in water. His fingertips hurt. Looking up from his hands, Yusuf saw Ace. The boy uttered a horrified sound.

Yusuf had seen it all. Now he couldn't see anything.

No matter what he did, he would never be able to do a single thing to save his brother.

• • •

DANA
The Next Morning

Being a police investigator meant being used to waking up at the crack of dawn. Dana stumbled into the bathroom to wash her face, her eyes murky with a fine film of discharge. Her hand groped around in the dark room for the light switch.

Coffee. I need coffee.

The bathroom illuminated. Dana was dead wrong. She didn't need caffeine to wake up. "Mark!" She howled.

"Wuhdoyouwan?" He muttered, sleep clouding his speech.

"Mark," Dana grasped the door frame to stop herself from sliding to her knees. "Mark, come *overhererightnow.*"

"What?" Mark appeared next to her. "Do you know what time–" His mouth stopped producing words. His jaw unhinged.

The hotel-provided first aid kit was torn open; bandages were uncoiled, toilet paper was unraveled, the EpiPen box was damp. An unzipped black backpack was tossed in the bathtub.

And flowering out on the white tiled ground was blood.

Someone could have injured themselves. They could have thrown up a cosmopolitan. Not that there were any to go around. But Dana knew none of the hypotheticals she thought up would be good enough to cover up the truth.

When she woke up, she didn't see Reid.

"Can you go any faster?" Dana prodded Mark again. She was clinging to the bottom of her seat for dear life already, but the quicker they found Reid the better.

"No can do," Mark responded, but he put more pressure on the gas pedal anyway.

"Are you sure he's going to be on this road?"

"Look, Dana," Mark slowed the vehicle down to a stop. He folded his hands over each other like he was praying and placed them over his mouth, exhaling deeply. "I know as much as you do," he said after a moment.

They sat in their shared worry for a while.

"Your brother's name is Ace, right?"

"Yeah."

"I hope he's okay. He looks like a smart young man."

Dana just nodded. Summer was supposed to be tiptoeing on beaches to avoid sharp rocks and shells, romantic flings, and red-white-and-blue fireworks. The air would taste like salt on your tongue if you lived close to the ocean, and it would be filled with sounds of cricket conductors conducting their cricket orchestra at night. This time of year wasn't supposed to be meeting ginger Scotsmen with pictures of your brother or search parties for a lost teenaged boy.

"Sometimes I want to leave," Mark said, breaking the silence.

"Leave what?"

"Vanessa is my spouse," he rubbed the back of his neck, grimacing. "We were supposed to get divorced yesterday but I showed up late for court." He wiped his bony hands on the front of his jeans before putting them back on the steering wheel. Mark sighed. "It's hard to give up a bad habit, but even harder when you infected it from someone you don't want to forget."

"What?"

Mark drew his hands from the leather ring and smashed them on the horn. Dana tensed, surprised at his actions. "Sorry," Mark blinked hard. "Ah, shit. Shit, sorry."

"It's okay."

"It's just that Vanessa annoys the hell out of me sometimes, you know? And I'm like a black hole, so she's pretty damn gifted to be able to piss me off," Mark laughed, sarcasm dripping from his sentences. "She has a little mental contamination OCD. She never explained how she got it or why she had it, which was probably my first red flag." He wiped the sweat condensing his hairline. "I should've taken it as a warning. If she couldn't trust me, how would *we* even work?"

Dana didn't say anything. She wanted to comfort Mark, but she didn't want him to think that she thought that he was begging for pity or sympathy. "We… Should probably get going, I guess. There's–"

"–Yeah. Yes." Mark sat up, cutting her off. He restarted her car and they took off once again.

"Stop," Dana gripped Mark's shoulder. "Stop, stop, stop!"

Lumped in a patch of grass was a pale figure wearing a torn sports jersey. Tangled hair framed a delicate, mud-smudged face. There was dried blood clumping a leg.

Mark hit the brakes. Dana scrambled to unbuckle her seatbelt. Whipping the car door open, she ran over to Reid.

Please let him be alive.

"Honey," she shook him. "Honey, wake up," she patted his cheek.

No response.

"Reid?" Mark joined in, hovering over the boy next to Dana.

Still no response.

"Oh my god," Dana whispered.

"Wait," Mark said. He gave Dana a knowing look. "We found Alexi."

"Alexi? What? Where?" Reid's eyelids flew open. He got up, wincing as he straightened his legs. "Where is she?"

"We were so worried!" Dana exclaimed, giving him a hug. "Are you okay?"

"Where's Alexi?"

"That was just to get you to wake up," Mark responded, climbing back into the car.

"Get in," Dana felt her heart unclench as she opened the backseat door for Reid, who limped inside.

She wondered what would happen if he hadn't waken up. Dana gulped, getting back into the shotgun side. What if it hadn't been Reid and it was Ace?

The engine roared back to life... And died down. They didn't have gas left. No way to get to her brother.

• • •

YUSUF
The Disappearance

Fresh red marks were slashed across his neck. His hair was poking out in several angles. The rims of his eyes were a dark hue of pink. Water beads clumped his eyelashes together. The bright studio lights illuminated him in a ghostly luster. Ace gaped at Yusuf in horror, his mouth quivering, unable to form a single word.

"Are you okay?" Yusuf whispered.

"Y-You tried to drown me," Ace stuttered, his face a contortion of sheer panic. He began to scramble out of the container to no avail when his feet kept slipping on the plastic.

"I–What?" Yusuf looked down at his hands. Sure enough, faint traces of blood and skin were soiling the underneath of his fingernails.

"Please don't kill me," Ace breathed, his back pressed against the container. He hugged his chest, trembling in the frigid water. "I don't want to die."

The cool waves lapped around Yusuf's waist. He began to remember things. The sound of his skin ripping when Ace scratched his forearm. Limbs tangling together, Ace's mouth gulping air. Yusuf hadn't been creating a sculpture–he was recreating the day he was in the bathtub. "Oh my god," he rasped. "Oh my god."

Ace was out of the water now, leaving blotches on the green paper. Jacob's drenched shirt shrank, glued to his skin. Yusuf followed him, shaking off the invisible tarantulas scampering up his body. They clung to the hem of his pants, unwilling to let go.

"Don't come near me," Ace growled at Yusuf, glaring at him. His irises were amber again, the hollow lines circling his pupil visible.

"Jacob," Yusuf gasped, rushing towards him. "Jacob, please don't go."

"It's too late," Memory-Jacob sighed, his rich, melanous skin fading into transparency.

Yusuf tried to grab his disappearing arm.

"Get away from me!" Ace shrieked, hurtling out of Yusuf's reach. He grabbed the wooden stool and held it out in front of his chest, the legs pointing at Yusuf.

Yusuf rammed his fingers into the sides of his head, yanking on his hair. His eyes were squeezed shut.

Come back.

A worrisome *bang!* exploded. Yusuf's eyelids fluttered open. Ace was smashing the doorknob with the mallet from Yusuf's toolbox, his head whipping back and forth to a state of unnerving alarm to check if Yusuf was getting closer.

Memory-Jacob neared the exit, his hand hesitating before he wrapped his fingers around the doorknob.

"Jacob," Yusuf cried, tears streaming down his yearning face. He fell down. He crawled towards his brother, his knees dragging on the floor. A nail that hadn't been hammered all the way down stabbed his kneecap, sending a wave of excruciation throughout his entire leg. He didn't care.

"You have to let me go," Memory-Jacob lamented.

Ace finally broke the doorknob. He shoved the door open.

"So long, you monster!" Ace screamed with every ounce of his might, free at last.

"I'm sorry," Memory-Jacob apologized. He twirled one of his raincoat strings, bouncing on the balls of his feet lightly. His eyes gazed at the pine thicket in front of the warehouse.

"No," Yusuf strained to get closer, but he couldn't. He was being held back by an unseen pressure that was shoving him away from the door. "No. No. Jacob, goddamnit, no!"

Memory-Jacob smiled a bittersweet smile.

Click.

The tension in his chest throbbed. Olympic backflips started in his stomach, along with a gagging feeling trapped at the end of his throat even though Yusuf wasn't choking. The quick succession of thoughts were released. *Hate Frank.* NO! *He killed your brother. It was his fault!* STOP IT! *What's Ace going to do now, huh? He's going to call the police and you're going to be sent to an asylum for the mentally diseased.* I AM NOT MY MENTAL DISORDER. There were teeth and claws suspending him to the ground, anticipating for him to give up. Tears pierced his burning face. Yusuf cradled himself on the ground, burrowing is head deep into the hole created by his arms and knees.

It's going to be okay, he chanted in his head, hoping it would override the mob jeering him. *It's going to be okay.*

The few minutes of hell passed slowly. Yusuf rose. He straightened his damp shirt, brushing off wood splinters that had attached themselves to it. Hesitating, he pushed open the entrance to the other room.

Frank was still in his seat, entertaining the remaining models.

"So, since you work with Yusuf, you must know what *untitled* is!" Alexi postulated.

"No, I actually don't," Frank replied. "I want to know what's underneath that old cloth as much as you do but that's one of Yusuf's individual projects. I don't meddle with those or else he gets real cranky," Frank noticed Yusuf. "God," he stood up, rushing over to him, speaking in a low tone so no one could hear. "You look like a mess."

"I'm fine," Yusuf croaked, tiptoeing a little to look over Frank's shoulder at Alexi. She wore a pensive expression on her face; her lips were twisted into a crooked grin but her eyes were chilling gray blanks. He turned to peek at Vanessa. She didn't look so different. Did they hear him in the studio?

"You need help, Yusuf," Frank urged, full of concern.

"No, really. I'm fine," Yusuf recited. But he wasn't, he honestly wasn't. He was just too sick of having to launch into the explanation of his whirlpool thought process. He couldn't watch as Frank tried to save him and fail another time. "Alexi?"

"Yeah?" She sat up straight.

"You're up next," Yusuf lead her into the studio.

Frank didn't budge after the girl went inside.

"I'm fine," Yusuf insisted. "I'm fine."

"Whoa," Alexi wandered around the room. She slid her fingers over the masking tape markings on the green screen wall. "This is cool. You wouldn't think such a…"

"Worn down?" Frank offered, chuckling to strengthen his disguise.

"Yeah," Alexi agreed. "This is so different compared the outside." She stepped back when the water began to seep into her shoes. "Where's Ace?" Her voice was thin.

"Ace had to leave early," Yusuf lied. It was so simple now, fibbing straight through his teeth. "Sorry about the mess. We had a little issue when we were taking the pictures and the water tank spilled."

He repositioned the camera and motioned for Alexi to come sit on the chair before the lens. He pushed down the metal hook of the second envelope, the one with "The Disappearance" written on it, and slid out this part of his journal. "The story behind your piece in this collection may sound straightforward, but the aftereffects aren't so pretty. Your face is going to be the highlight. I want to capture it corrupted in a look of agony. You're going to be the face of a girl who went missing."

Alexi clutched onto the edge of her chair. "Missing," she enunciated the adjective as if she were unsure. "Did it actually happen?"

Yusuf avoided meeting Alexi's questioning ogle. "Yes. Quite a while ago." His hand fell from readjusting the tripod. "The police held so many search parties," he struggled to get out. "It was on every newspaper in the town."

"That's sad."

"It still is," Yusuf cleared his throat. "I'll need you to stay very still," Yusuf told Alexi, who was squirming in her seat. "Do you have any questions before we start?"

"Yeah," she glanced at the table beside him. "What are those?" She asked the pile of Plaster of Paris strips.

"Have you ever broken a bone before?"

Alexi nodded with a wince as if remembering how much it hurt, but then she laughed. "Yeah, it was so dumb."

"This is Plaster of Paris," Yusuf picked up one of the pieces, white powder puffing out from it. "You dip it in water," he sloshed it around for a brief second until it dissolved into a limp cloth with a glue-like consistency. "And you wrap it around whatever you want to." He placed the wet strip on her exposed shoulder.

"Ew," Alexi chuckled, smoothing her fingers over it. "It's sticky. And kinda cold." The white residue caked her fingers.

"Here," Yusuf handed her a damp rag. "You'll want to wipe that–"

The gold decals on her paisley shirt flashed underneath the glow of the studio lights. It was Clara's–cut up and sewn without much thought on a regular T-shirt.

"Wipe it off," Yusuf continued, swallowing. "The longer you wait, the harder it'll get." A jolt of electricity shocked him when she took the rag from him, and not the type when you make a connection with someone. It rippled through him like he stuck a wet finger into an electrical socket.

"Hey, are you–"

Yusuf was slipping. Reality had no grasp on him and he had no grasp on it. The field of fresh grass dotted with dew was back under his feet. Alexi's voice slurred, vibrating a mechanical pitch. She began to split into pieces–her legs became thick trees, feathers pierced through from her arms, transforming into birds, her head morphed into the sun. At last, only her torso was left. It shrank, dropping down until it hovered mere inches above the green. Then it changed. Steel blue moccasins belonging to a pair of dainty feet were nestled in the grass. A necklace was hanging from a thick neck. Sticky, popsicle juice-stained fingers grabbed Yusuf's hands, pulling him forward.

"Play with me."

The bars keeping his metal heart prisoner crashed down in the blink of an eye. "Clara," Yusuf babbled, going weak. "Clara, baby."

"Play with me," she repeated, swaying with the tall grass. A pink and golden sunset overlooked them, making wisps of her ink black hair sparkle. "Run, daddy!" She took off, tripping and zig-zagging like a ditz through the field. "Don't let them catch you!"

"Who's them?" Yusuf asked, slowing down to keep up with her.

Instead of breathing like someone normally would, Clara opened her mouth as wide as she could and let the air fill it, making her look like a child-sized chipmunk. "Them..." Clara trailed off as she ran even harder, stomping the ground with such force the grass cleared a path for her wherever she went. "Them is Them. Do you know who Them is?"

They reached the edge of the cliff.

"Be careful now," Yusuf captured her cozy palm. Just then did he realize how much he missed doing that.

"Do you know who Them is, daddy?" She said again in that innocent way little kids did, but something about her voice seemed off. It felt like she was captured in a trance.

"I don't think I know, sweetheart. Why don't you tell me?"

Her small hands tucked fabric of her paisley dress underneath her plump little bottom before she sat down at the edge of the field like Angie taught her to.

"Careful there," Yusuf said, pulling Clara closer to him. It was a good thing that she was short. If she had been any taller, her ears would be level with his chest. It was a good thing. Yusuf didn't want to spook her with how fast his pulse was.

"Sit beside me, okay?" He scooted even further back, patting the patch of grass beside him.

"I want to touch the sun, daddy," Clara announced with a firm nod of her head, the mysterious Them all forgotten.

"I think it would like your company very much." Yusuf got up and wrapped his arms around her waist, hoisting her up so she could have a better view of the glowing ball that shined before them.

"Really? Can I go–WHEE!"

Yusuf lifted Clara up in the air and spun her around until he was lightheaded and close to toppling off the edge.

"More!" Clara shrieked with delight as Yusuf put her down.

"I can't," he chuckled, stroking her tresses. "I'm getting too dizzy."

They stared into the distance, as the sky grew darker, pulling all its vivid colors with it. Yusuf felt infinite.

"Do you miss Uncle Jacob?" Clara mumbled, drowsy in his lap.

"I do, very much."

"Daddy?"

"Yes, sweetie?"

"I'm sorry," she wrapped her grubby fingers around the hem of sweatpants, rubbing the plush material against his cheek. "For breaking your person."

"Oh," Yusuf said. About a week ago, Clara accidentally broke the sculpture he had been working on for a long time. Yusuf bristled, despite the warm weather. He had yelled at Clara, screamed at her with all the voice he had. "It's okay."

Clara peered at Yusuf, her Stygian black eyes sparkling with teardrops. "Are you angry at me, daddy?"

A pang of guilt struck him in his chest. "No, of course, I'm not angry," Yusuf reassured her, but he wasn't telling the truth. He was angry. He was furious. That sculpture had been his life. Now it wasn't even in it anymore. But just by seeing Clara and her rosy cheeks and her wobbly smile, Yusuf melted. "Don't worry, okay, sweetheart? I'm not angry."

Clara was fast asleep in his lap, her breathing gentle and calm.

This is what she must've looked like when they took her, a voice speculated in his head. *Tucked away in her blankets with no idea that the moment she woke up, she wouldn't be–*

"No!" A panicked squeal erased the field.

"Clara!" Yusuf shrieked. She was dissipating. Her bronze skin darkened. It was flaking into ashes, flying towards Yusuf like a horde of crows.

"Don't hurt me!" The voice wailed.

He was in an empty, white void now. There was no beginning and no end to it and everything was gone. Yusuf collapsed. He didn't hold on tight enough.

Something cold and hard dug into his palm. He opened his hands. Amidst a mound of soot was the pendant on Clara's necklace. "Clara… Clara…" Yusuf hugged the piece of singed metal close to him, a waterfall of tears freefalling past his face. "Clara!"

All of a sudden, his lower half erupted. The void cleared back into the settings of his art studio. "Aaargh!" He bellowed, sinking to the ground with his hands cupped around the family jewels.

"Lesson one: you don't mess with me," Alexi held his stomach down with her foot.

Yusuf felt like he was going to die.

"Is this what you tried to do to Ace?" Alexi interrogated him. She snatched his tripod by its legs and smashed the camera strapped to the top. Yusuf heard glass shattering. "Try to strangle him to death?"

Yusuf managed to catch a glimpse of Alexi. The necklace she was wearing that had belonged to Clara was nowhere to be found. In its place were scratches. Short, gristly ones covering Alexi from the shoulders and above. Blood was smeared across her face, fingerprints imprinted in the crimson. His. Yusuf's gaze trailed to the ground. The necklace was strewn across the broken camera, its chain snapped into half. The tip of the pendant was red.

"You disgust me," Alexi spat. She leaned down and delivered a slap that stung his cheek. "Shame on you, Yusuf Bates. I hope you rot in hell." She pushed the door open and marched out in triumph.

"I was trying to save her," Yusuf groaned on the floor, but he was too quiet for Alexi to hear.

Clara's necklace glinted in the piercing studio lights.

They were no longer memories. They were here.

CHAPTER TWELVE

YUSUF
Number of Hours Until SculptFest: Five

Knock knock knock.

"Yusuf?" Frank called.

Yusuf groaned, his left hand numb from the glass shards chasing blood out from under his skin. He was a fully grown man, not some child who needed a parent to take care of him twenty-four-seven. "Who died and made you king?" He mumbled, still on the ground.

"Yusuf?" Frank questioned again like he wasn't sure what his best friend's name was. "Yus—"

"STOP IT," Yusuf said. He didn't shout like he had before; he spoke with a loudness that commanded attention. He was in control now.

"Wha—"

"STOP IT, STOP IT, *STOP IT,*" Yusuf left no pauses in between to let Frank talk. He squeezed his eyes shut for darkness but received a scarlet glare instead. Spirals of his ebony hair tickled the sides of his face, coaxing the sweat beads on his forehead to drip down. Grease oiled the curves and layers of his body. The only sounds in the studio were Yusuf's panting breaths and the flickering of a dying light bulb.

The door flew open. Yusuf knew exactly what was going to happen. First, Frank was going to observe. His heartbeat would quicken at the mere sight of water drenching the floorboards, the cuts of glass scattered on the ground, the splashes of blood decorating the studio. Next, he was going to rush to Yusuf. Ask him if he was okay. Ask what on earth happened in here. Then he was going to drag Yusuf's ass to therapy and make him suffer through years of candlelit sessions of a "doctor" bullshitting on and on about how he had to forgive himself while classical string quartet music played in the background. Over his dead body, he would.

His mental disorder was not beautiful. It was not an attention-driven kamikaze mission. It was not a plea for sympathy.

It was something that demanded understanding. Listening.

"Yu–"

"Shut up," Yusuf leaped up, wincing at the shooting pains racing through his body. "I'm not doing anything you ask anymore. No more questions." He trod towards Frank, who was wide-eyed with shock for a split second until he realized that Yusuf was targeting him like a bull charging at a red cloth.

"Calm down."

"I'm calm!"

"I just wanted to know whether you're done with the photos yet so we can work on the sculptures," Frank got out before Yusuf could interrupt him again.

"Oh," Yusuf replied. His hand was still burning with blood. The studio lights didn't help. "Huh."

Frank's poker face didn't budge. It was a blessed curse; Yusuf could never tell if Frank was truly ignorant or plotting a giant master plan.

"So?"

"Right," Yusuf scratched his head. "I just need one more photo…" He trailed off when he remembered that Alexi had smashed his camera to smithereens. "Yeah. This one's going to require a different setting so Vanessa and I might be heading out."

"Okay," Frank said, slipping out of the studio.

He didn't sleep that night. Vanessa didn't look so comfortable either when he introduced the idea of sleeping on a spare mattress to her.

The shadows cast by the stripes of light filtering in through the blinds were long, signaling the beginning of the late morning. "Good morning," Yusuf closed the door to the studio.

"Hello," Vanessa replied, swinging her feet off the metal footrest running around the legs of the stool to stand up. The corners of her mouth curved into a smile that didn't expose her teeth. Her stance was cautious, one hand on the back of the chair. She had heard the commotion yesterday, Yusuf was sure of it. Maybe not everything, but just enough to be suspicious.

Yusuf pinched the two flaps sealing the final envelope shut to open it. "The sculpture you will be modeling for is titled *The Separation.* I'm going to take a few photos of your hand." He tapped the yellow cardstock against his palm to shake an item out.

Vanessa's pale face turned even paler.

"You're going to be wearing this." Yusuf held a delicate rose gold circle. Elegant twin swirls dotted with diamonds framed the star of the show: a peach sapphire.

It was Angie's wedding ring.

•••

REID
Summer Vacation: Day Three

They sat on the curbside, doing nothing. "Why do we have to wait?" Reid groaned.

"Because if we go to wherever this address leads to, we could put everyone's lives in jeopardy."

"What's wrong with you?" Reid asked, kicking a stone into the drain across from them. "We already checked that off our list of ridiculous things to do during the summer."

"We're out of gas," Mark reminded him in the calmest voice Reid had heard him speak in throughout the entire trip. It was so hot his hair was dripping with sweat. "And I don't want to find out how long it takes us to get there by foot."

"We could call the police. Police help people."

"Do you want to make this more complicated than it already is? Do you know how much longer it would take to get to your friend or her brother," Mark jabbed his finger in Dana's direction, "or whoever if we got the force involved?"

Reid laughed, his face red with fury. "*Dana's* in the force! You want us just to sit on the side of the road like what, hitchhikers, and do nothing?"

Mark pushed himself to a standing position, his stinky plaid shirt balled up in his hands. "Yes."

Adrenaline shocked his veins, threatening to burst. Reid leaped up. His bruised hands curled into fists, his fingernails digging into his wounds.

"Don't," Dana said in a hushed tone before Reid could whip Mark with his fury.

But–"

"Sit down."

"I need to–"

"No. Sit down. Both of you," Dana whispered, fire charring the ends of her words.

They sat. The wind whipped the trees back and forth, sprinkling dried-up leaves on the ground. Reid watched the sunlight bounce off his plastic water bottle.

His imagination had abandoned him, refusing to populate his head with radiant fantasies like it used to be able to do.

Alexi could be dead right now. Dead. She could actually be dead. Bile crept up, using his the back of his throat as a stepladder. Alexi. Rest in peace, deceased, passed away, *dead*. Her body still on filthy ground. A pool of blood would frame her pretty face, electrified with terror. Her stormy gray eyes would be wide open, filled with fading optimism as maggots started to breed and her skin began to peel away. The oversized shirt she had been wearing would be ripped apart at the seams, her short shorts would be scrunched up. One of her sneakers would be missing.

Reid dug his fingernails into his palms.

She could have been raped. Threatened at gunpoint. Forced to act against her will. "I need to go," he grabbed his water and began to sprint down the road. "I need to go find her."

"No, you're not," Mark held the back of Reid's jersey collar before he could get anywhere. "You already went once and–"

"No." Reid writhed out of his grasp, tearing the material with a sound *rrrrp.* "No. She needs me. I need her. I need to go." He tried to run away, but Mark's grip on his arms was too strong. "Let me go!"

Silence.

"LET ME GO!" Reid's screams echoed in the forest. He was not about to sit around and wait for the one person who made his life worth living. He was going to find Alexi and beat the shit out of whoever hurt her. His right foot kicked Mark's shin. Mark buckled to the asphalt, holding his leg in pain.

"Stop!" Reid heard Dana cry. She chased after him, but Reid was too fast for her. He thundered forward, the pine trees and scarlet toadstools blurs of nothing.

Then he stopped. He stopped because he was tackled onto the grass, two arms with fresh bruise marks strung around his neck, a pair of legs hooked around his waist. A heartbeat that belonged to someone he knew pounded quick and hard.

And. They. Burned. Like. A. Million. Bonfires.

"Oh my god," Alexi whispered, her face pressed against the back of his neck. Her glasses poked him. The peachy scent Reid had memorized was replaced with the faint bitterness of blood. She was sweating grime out of her pores and her words were barely coherent, but Reid couldn't give less of a damn about any of that right now. She was alive.

"I can't breathe."

"Oh," Alexi chuckled. "Sorry."

Reid flipped around and sat up so they were across from each other.

Alexi was staring at him, her big doe eyes welling up with tears that jerked his heartstrings. She covered her mouth with both hands. Indistinct pink lines that look like the work of a necklace scarred the valley of her collarbones and neck. Her shirt was torn at the shoulder, leaving one of her arms bare.

Reid broke down.

Alexi was his gold. He would never leave her, ever.

"Are you okay?" He managed to choke out between snorts and the stream of tears raining down his flushed cheeks.

"I'm okay," Alexi leaned forward and hugged him tightly.

Reid didn't think anything in the world could feel this good. "Hey," he said when they pulled away.

Alexi wiped a few tears of her own from her face. Her nose was pink, matching the color of her lips. She was smiling so wide that Reid could see the outline of her teeth in her gums. "You're my bean."

"I'm your bean," Alexi laughed, blinking away incoming tears. "You're my bean too." She lost it. "Oh god, I thought I'd never see you again," she dove in for another hug, drenching Reid's shirt.

After a moment, they stood up and brushed the dirt and grass off their knees. "I'm with some people. We should probably go to them," Reid told Alexi as they headed towards Dana and Mark. He didn't say that Dana was an investigator. By the looks of it, Alexi was in no mood to talk about what had happened. It didn't matter. *She's here. She's with me.*

"Okay."

"Hey," Reid grinned, sliding his hand down from her shoulder to cradle her waist. Pulling her closer to him, he planted a quick kiss on her cheek. "Fuck the odds, you're alive."

The tip of Alexi's ears blushed. "Charming. Sweaty, but charming."

After Reid introduced Alexi to Mark and Dana and Dana and Mark to Alexi, the four of them sat on the grass.

"What should we do now?" Dana broke the silence.

"I thought you had the answers to everything," Mark simpered.

Dana rolled her eyes.

"Ooh, look at the lovebirds," Alexi whispered into Reid's ear with a giggle. Their fingers were intertwined.

"Oh shut up, they met, like, a day ago." But Reid could see the bond the two adults had. It wasn't romantic, like what Alexi suggested. Instead, it looked like the beginning of an alliance.

"You lads should get someplace safer than here," Mark said. "We're still looking for people so we'll stay out here."

"I'll call the police," Dana unzipped her bag and took out her phone. Mark didn't object.

"So I guess this is goodbye then," Reid faced Mark when Dana was a little further away. "Thanks for helping us." He meant it. Although Mark was one of the most sarcastic assholes he had met, he wasn't all that bad. They shook hands.

"Take good care of your friend," Mark advised him, nodding at Alexi, who was still clasping Reid's palm. Ow. The girl had a *really* strong grip. "And take good care of yourself, yeah?"

"Yeah."

"Bruce?" Dana exclaimed, a few feet away. "Wow, I had no idea you worked in this part of town." Pause. "We're kind of in the forest. There's only one road so you'll probably be able to find us," Dana affirmed. "Okay. See you soon." She hung up. "A colleague of mine is going to pick you two up soon. It turns out the police station is really close to here, just behind the woods."

"Cool."

"Reid," Dana motioned for Reid to come with her to a more disclosed part of the thicket. "Stay safe okay, honey? Make sure to listen to your parents."

"Ugh," Reid rolled his eyes. If he had listened to his mom, he wouldn't be here right now.

"I know, I know. But trust me, it's good advice," Dana told him. Her purse vibrated. "One sec," she picked up. "Hello?" There was a pregnant pause. "What?" Her jaw went slack. "Are you sure? Oh my god." She stood up, ending the call.

"They found Ace."

• • •

YUSUF
The Separation

"I can't," Vanessa blinked. She edged away from the wedding ring in Yusuf's palm.

Upon meeting her for the first time, she seemed like any other person at any other art exhibit. But now, through the red veins invading the whites of her eyes, Yusuf saw. He saw sadness that had been ignored by everyone else who had crossed paths with her.

Yusuf waited for Vanessa to elaborate. Partly because he didn't know what to say, but also partly because his subconscious wanted to hear her voice stripped down to raw vulnerability. It was corrupted, but he wanted to hear someone's pain. It made him feel like he wasn't alone.

"I was supposed to get divorced yesterday. My spouse didn't show up."

"Oh," Yusuf rubbed her shoulder with empathy, all the wants of listening to her tortured voice gone. "I'm so sorry. Really. I'm divorced myself. And hey, if it helps you, the sculpture you're modeling is called *The Separation*. I think you could relate a lot to it."

"What's it about?"

Yusuf smiled an acidic smile at Vanessa. "Empty spaces in between relationships when you don't know what to do with yourself. That feeling when you leave, or the person who loves you leaves." But couldn't that be the same person? Yusuf wondered.

Maybe the closure of a relationship meant closure with a part of yourself.

"Face it," a voice that didn't belong to Vanessa said.

Yusuf whipped around. Standing at the exit of the warehouse was a woman. She wore a butterscotch colored tunic top, jeans that clung to her waist and bagged over her legs. Her skin was a gorgeous espresso. A bracelet of twine circled her wrist, a minuscule bronze-gold medallion attached to the string. She had no face. Replacing her features were newspaper scraps wrapped in the shape of her head, dipping to form her eyes, curving to make up her nose. They all said the same things:

November 16, 2008.

I want to touch the sun, daddy.

But there was an addition to the newspapers that Yusuf had never seen before–a tree. It wasn't printed on the paper. It was sprouting from her shoulders, filling the hollows of her necks with thick roots.

"It's over, Yusuf," Angie whispered with her headline-covered mouth, her kinky brown hair drooping. Her tongue and teeth were constructed of black and white text too. "I can't do this."

"Why?" Yusuf asked, taking gentle steps towards her.

Angie didn't respond.

The crisp summer air flowed in through the door as she opened it, dragging a blue hard shell suitcase with her. "Thank you," Angie mouthed, pulling off the wedding band off her finger and tossing it to the ground. It landed with a delicate *clink*.

"No," Yusuf lunged towards her, grabbing the ring. He tried to touch her hand and force it back on, but when he made contact, her skin became the headlines. "Angie," he tugged her suitcase. The words kept spreading, bleeding onto the ground, wherever anything made a movement. "Don't go."

Angie stopped. She turned around. Her face was bare of the newspaper now, and Yusuf melted at the sight of her eyes–two black abysses. "Keep believing in Clara," she whispered. Her legs thickened into one, her smooth skin becoming rough and chipped. Twigs grew out of her arms, small green leaves budding. Her eyes became hollow. She had become a tree. Then she began to decompose and wilt until she was nothing but a mound of dirt. A single blade of grass poked through.

It didn't keep growing.

"Where are we going?" Vanessa asked, still nursing her finger.

Yusuf cringed, remembering how limp her bones felt when he wrapped gauze and medical tape around it. According to Vanessa, he had tripped while slipping the ring on her and yanked her down with him, spraining her finger. He had a feeling that that wasn't the case. "A place I haven't been in a long time."

They pulled up to a house. The roof had rust red shackles layering it, a gray brick chimney with soot at its mouth. The front door was a pine green that matched the forest. The residents' name was painted in neat block letters on the dented metal mailbox: Bates. Yusuf headed towards the broken white fence, ignoring Vanessa's questions. He stepped across the damaged wood, going straight into the backyard. The familiar scent of peonies waltzed to his nose before he got there. A gunshot of melancholy pierced his chest. Long weeds had poked their way out of the dirt. The burial place was abundant with moss. Tiny black ants scurried in and out of minuscule holes.

Yusuf took out his switchblade from his pants pocket and yanked the bunches of crabgrass up slightly so he could hack them off at the roots. He scraped the dirt away and dug until he found what he was looking for.

Inside that damp cardboard box that had been buried years ago was his daughter.

"Hello, Clara," Yusuf lifted the lid open gently. "I missed you."

"Hello," she replied.

CHAPTER THIRTEEN

FRANK
Number of Hours Until SculptFest: Two

Someone knocked on the door. "Investigator Bruce. Is there a Frank Cavallero here?"

Frank's pulse stopped. And started again. "Yes," he opened the door. "I'm Frank."

A man with broad shoulders and abundant arm hair stood there with a fleet of cops wearing stern expressions. "Someone has reported that a man who lives with you under the name of Yusuf Bates has harmed a twenty-year-old and a fifteen-year-old innocent. Is this statement true?"

Frank remembered the loud *whomp* in the studio just moments after Ace went inside. The distressed cries. How the young college student never came back to learn the fate of that poor little hamster. Alexi never came back either. "I-I can't say."

A tall person with unruly dark auburn curls loitered behind Investigator Bruce. Tied around his waist was an unbuttoned plaid shirt that looked like it had gone without a wash for one too many days. His eyes were empty. It was Mark

"Do you live with Mr. Bates?"

"Yes, I do," Frank replied, swallowing nonexistent saliva.

"Were you aware of any dangerous activities he might have been doing?"

"No–I mean, I don't know."

Investigator Bruce exhaled, beads of sweat dotting his bald head. If he stayed out any longer without getting a hat, he would get a nasty sunburn on his scalp. "Do you have any evidence you think might help us?"

"No," Frank began to reply, but then the lightbulb in his head lit up. "Yes." He disappeared back into the warehouse for a second to get the notebook. As he unzipped his chunk of a backpack, he felt the glare of the studio lights stare at him.

Hand over the polaroids, they said.

No. If there was one thing he couldn't give up, it was those three polaroids. He grabbed the notebook and returned to the investigator, passing it over to him.

"Thank you for your time."

"Not a problem. Goodbye."

When the door closed, Frank dashed into the studio. Ignoring the glass smithereens and the crimson painting the room with guilt, he flew out the back door.

He reached the bus depot. It was time to drive Bus 59 to its final destination.

CHAPTER FOURTEEN

YUSUF
The Separation

After Yusuf found Clara, he decided he needed to one last thing before going to the competition. He needed to go to the lake. He didn't know why he wanted to, he just had to. They pulled up to the meadow.

At this time of the year, it was common for it to be hot and sticky from dusk to dawn, but it wasn't at this moment. The weather was a strange chill, something Yusuf didn't expect during the summer. The rustic pine thicket unfolded behind the silent waters; the ashen sky painting the evening faded yellow and dust gray. To anyone else, this place looked like any other spread of nature–moss blanketing rocks and dried-up tree roots. To Yusuf, it was a nightmare. The faint odor of algae alone made the back of his throat ache, and not because it smelled bad.

Yusuf spread two metal chairs on the soft grass in silence, dew beads clinging to his leg hairs. "Please," he motioned at one of them. "Take a seat."

Vanessa hesitated before sitting down. She was still clutching her left ring finger.

Yusuf stared at Clara in his lap.

"You can do it," she smiled.

Yusuf swallowed the repugnant lump in his throat. "I brought you here because I owe you an explanation," he started.

"It's rude not to look at someone when you speak," Vanessa cut in with a surprisingly strong voice.

Yusuf's eyes met hers. "Eight years ago, I was supposed to get married to the loves of my life. Two weeks before the wedding, Frank and my brother–"

"Frank as in Frank the sculptor, Frank the bus driver, Frank?"

"Yes," Yusuf paused. He was trembling. "In November, Frank and my brother went out one evening to plan my bachelor party. But the ground was layered with sleet and ice and somehow Frank lost control of the car. They crashed," Yusuf mellowed, his gaze drifting elsewhere. "Into this lake. My brother drowned to death." It was vicious–how instead of celebrating the new life of two, they mourned the end of one.

A form flickered on top of the serene waters. A man with a tan fur-lined coat and a head of black hair appeared. It was Jacob. Two eel-like creatures were wrapped around his legs, brown slime oozing from their scales.

"Goodbye, Jacob," Yusuf whispered through his teeth.

The animals snapped their jaws shut, sinking their razor teeth into his brother. Dark blood trickled down like a leaking faucet. Soon enough, the water became an alarming shade of red. But Jacob didn't scream or move or say anything. His face was expressionless as the creatures dragged him down into the lake. Right before he disappeared for good, Yusuf saw Jacob's mouth curve into his boyish smile.

"Are you okay?" Vanessa's question shattered his daze.

"I'm fine," Yusuf replied, meaning it this time. "Shortly after my brother passed, my daughter disappeared."

"Keep going," Clara egged him on from inside her box. Yusuf could almost feel her warm face burrowed into his shoulder when they shared their last hug.

"I miss you so much, baby," tears stung his eyes as he imagined running his fingers through soft ebony curls. He yearned to hold the back of her bicycle so she wouldn't fall off, read her bedtime stories.

One more moment.

Taking a second to breathe, Yusuf continued. "Then my wife and I got divorced. There was no reason behind it. Sometimes things don't work out and they don't need pros or cons or motives at all."

His truck rumbled to life. It belonged to Angie after a drunken bet during their college years with a friend. "You're right," Angie said, her hands leaving the steering wheel. And just like that, she disintegrated into dust.

The haze cleared as the last rays of the sunset vanished behind the forest. "I buy the same bouquet of white lilies for my brother's grave every time the last bunch has died. I'm unable to look at the sunset without breaking a little because it reminds me of my daughter. My fourth finger on my left hand doesn't have a tan line around it anymore. I have to live going to the flower shop once a month. I avoid going outside when it's dusk. It makes me hurt because I don't have to worry about losing my wedding band when washing the dishes." Yusuf paused. "And that's okay."

• • •

MARK
The Farewell

He was still sitting in the waiting room of the Bronton Township police station. Dana, Reid, Ace, and Alexi had left. Curious murmurs trickled in through the crack in the sliding glass window where the police were behind.

Would you like a blanket? One of the officers had asked him.

No, dumbass, Mark had wanted to say. *It's ninety degrees outside and I'm not in shock. I'm just tired.* But instead, he just said, *no, thank you.*

The black door barricading Mark from the interior of the headquarters kept swinging open and closed. Officers went in and out to ask him questions he didn't know the answers to.

How did you get the location of the warehouse?

Frank gave it to me.

Do you have any connections with him or Yusuf Bates?

No.

Do you know any of the people in these photographs?

Yes.

Is there anything you can tell us?

Yes. He wanted to get the hell out of here.

But Mark stayed because he knew that Vanessa would end up here sooner or later. Although they weren't together anymore, he needed for her to see him when she got to the police station. Not because he wanted to make her feel better or because he wanted to know if she was okay. Mark just wanted to say goodbye.

The trigger of their divorce was a fight. There was no yelling. No clichéd throwing of vases. There was silence, locked doors. Vanessa couldn't "stand our differences" and Mark thought they were "meant for each other since day one" and they couldn't "give up based on these little things we do that irritate each other". Vanessa had moved out of their confined apartment and a few days later, she had called Mark and told him they were getting separated.

Loving someone had its consequences. You cannot give and give and give, because they will take and take and take. They lose interest in keeping the relationship alive. They stop trying.

Tap tap tap, said the windowpane behind him.

Mark turned around.

Luscious pink lips with a sweet dip in their cupid's bow smiled with a hint of sadness.

Mark slipped out of the station. Vanessa stood next to the brick wall exterior. A bush sprouted near her feet. Her ring finger, which Mark noticed right away, was not bare. It was dressed in a layer of gauze. He didn't ask questions.

"I am not going inside," Vanessa said in a tone that clearly stated *don't interrupt.* "I am going to the hospital because I think my finger may be broken. Then I am going home. Then we are getting our divorce finalized on Friday morning at eight o'clock sharp and you're damn right if you think we're still getting separated if you don't show up like last time." With a cold stare trapped in her eyes, Vanessa began to walk away.

"Wait," Mark called. He scrunched his shirt in his hands harder. She was the only person who could make him feel nervous like this.

Vanessa stopped in her tracks.

"It was the highlight of my mid-twenties to get to know you," he said.

Vanessa tucked a strand of her wavy hair behind her ear. "It was the highlight of my mid-twenties to get to know you as well," Vanessa replied. "But I'm not sorry we had to end. It's the universe that's pushing us apart and you can't argue with the universe."

"You can't," Mark agreed.

The slow summer wind whooshed, ruffling their clothes. Mark caught a glimpse of Vanessa's other birthmark pigmented on the back of her thigh.

"I hope we continue as friends sometime in the future," Vanessa added as she started to head down the desolate road again.

"I hope so too."

"Bye, Mark."

Mark loosened his grip on his shirt.

"Bye, Vanessa."

CHAPTER FIFTEEN

YUSUF
SculptFest

He pulled up to the competition in his red pickup truck.

"Are you ready?" He turned to Clara.

"If you are."

Yusuf hoisted her up and together, they got out of the vehicle.

"Showtime," a person wearing a headset alerted him. "You ready?"

It was a hurricane backstage–dark and jittery, artists bustling around, some painting on final layers of glaze, some rehearsing their speeches. If this were any other year of SculptFest, Yusuf would've felt a swarm of butterflies brewing in his stomach.

The stagehand drew back the velvet curtains to let Yusuf on. "You're on in ten seconds."

In the corner of his eye, Yusuf saw Frank rushing towards him, doused in sweat and sheer trepidation. He was surprised for a brief moment, but then his surprise boiled into anger. He was not going to be Frank's puppet anymore. He was not going to pretend that he didn't have any demons haunting him. He wanted to display them without a single ounce of shame.

"Before we announce the winner of SculptFest 2016, we still have one last entry," the presenter addressed the audience in a thundering voice. She swept her blonde hair extensions back. "Give it up for two of our returning sculptors–"

Frank thrust his hand out trying to pull Yusuf back, but a security guard patrolling the area blocked him. "I'm one of them!" He yelled, flailing in the man's grip on his shoulders. His black eyes glinted when splinters of the stage lights hit them.

Yusuf started to climb the plywood stairs leading up to the main platform.

"Yusuf!" Frank called, struggling past the guard, "come back!"

Yusuf couldn't even find the energy to say "no" anymore. Blinding white lights illuminated him when he was on the stage. The sea of audience roared. They were cheering for him, but their affection began to simmer down when they realized there wasn't a second man on stage. Yusuf ignored them, walking to where the microphone stood.

"Good luck, daddy!" Clara beamed from inside her cardboard box.

"Yusuf!"

He whipped around.

Frank was at the foot of the stage entrance, trying to get away from the two broad-shouldered men who held him back.

Yusuf couldn't move.

Kicking free, Frank crawled onto the podium.

Go. Yusuf had to go.

The crowd held their breath.

With Frank running towards him and the judges waiting, there was nothing left to do except for the inevitable:

Yusuf smashed Clara onto the stage.

Her thin Plaster of Paris shell cracked in half, smithereens of white puffing up into the night upon impact like a smoke bomb.

The audience gasped, confused murmurs filling the quiet indigo sky.

Frank stopped in his tracks.

Yusuf smiled. Right here, right now, he was transcendent. Even though he went to the flower shop to buy the same bouquet of white lilies for his brother's grave every time the last bunch died, despite being unable to admire the sunset without breaking a little because it reminded him of his daughter, although his ring finger on his left hand didn't have a tan line around it anymore, he was free.

The past and the future were two different halves. But just because the line isolating them was blurry at times, it didn't mean he had to choose which one to live in.

He knew how to find the calm in the midst of his hurricane now.

THE END

EPILOGUE

I'm a gumball machine, half empty and forgotten in the middle of
a mall.
You're a person, too scared to be vulnerable about anything at
all.
You turn the metal handle–that's your first shot.
And I make it worth the coin you slipped through the little slot.

You keep grinding the handle, but I'm running out of candy.
I'm more than happy to give, it's just that I think you see me as
an object that comes in handy.
Your visits used to be rare, one piece was enough to keep you
going.
Now you come
as if I were addicting.

I haven't told you before, but you should already know–
gumball machines grow old.
Sometimes I don't know how to give you your treat.
You curse and spit, kicking me, shaking me, begging me for
one more sweet.
I give it to you. It's not the flavor you wanted.

Over the course of time, you give up on me.
I give up on you.
Sometimes I wonder if you go to another gumball machine.
Sometimes I wonder if you have run out of coins to dispense.
Your choices are *not* at my expense.

I should've given you the right gumball. I'm sorry.
You don't come see me anymore–how are you doing?
Then I find you. Your mouth is chewing.
The taste isn't from me, but I'm glad it makes you happy.

ACKNOWLEDGEMENTS

A big thank you and lots of love go to my parents for supporting me this entire hell of a ride. Thanks for taking me to publishing houses without a pitch, bringing me to book signings, and helping me when I don't know what to do. I love you!

We are 9,567 miles away from each other, but you are still two of my biggest cheerleaders. Thank you, Oli and Owen, for answering all my weird questions and always listening. You guys are the best. I miss you so much!

A shoutout to all the authors and teachers who have responded to my emails and taught me lessons I'll never forget. Your advice never fails to save me on my bad writing days.

My fellow writers and friends on social media–thank you for encouraging me whenever I doubt myself and congratulating me when I succeed. The writing community is something I'm incredibly honored to be a part of.

And you. You are one heck of a reader if you're still with me. I hope you love this book as much as I do. It means the world to me that you welcomed my novel into your life. Thank you, thank you, thank you!

ABOUT THE AUTHOR

Mel Ingrid is a person who loves writing so much that she decided she wanted it to stay in her life for as long as humanly possible. Her first full-length novel is a YA psychological thriller titled BUS 59 AND A HALF.

If you reference BBC's *Sherlock* or *Inception* at any point, she will lose her mind in the best way. Mel also adores dogs, listening to alternative music, and snacks.

Born in Long Island, New York, Mel was raised by loving Taiwanese parents and evening walks on the neighborhood beach. When she was in the first grade, she and her family moved halfway across the world to Singapore, where she resided for seven years. She now writes and procrastinates in New Jersey.

If you want to find out more about Mel, you can follow her on Instagram (@mel_ingrid.writer), visit her website: www.melingrid.wordpress.com, or check out her GoodReads.

Perhaps you have a question or comment for her. In that case, you can message her through any of her platforms. She would be more than delighted to respond to you.

Printed in Great Britain
by Amazon